THE CRYSTAL KINGDOM

NEW YORK TIMES and USA TODAY
BESTSELLING AUTHOR
MILLY TAIDEN

ABOUT THE BOOK

Running is Chelsea Golby's escape. Literally. She runs to get away from the pain of being rejected after asking the love of her life to marry her. Instead of wallowing in self-pity, or a pint of Ben and Jerry's, she heads to the Crystal Kingdom to hang out with her sister Avery, the new Elf Queen. With Avery busy being queen, she decides to go on a run to see the magical lands. Maybe what her grandmom said was true and Chelsea has magic in her blood too.

Zaos Firefoot,the right hand man to King Gorwin, knows his people are fading out. It's too bad he can't tell the dumb-ass leader exactly what he thinks about how he rules the kingdom. As much as he hates it, Zaos does what he's told. Until the day he's sent out to question and kill a light elf. When Zaos finds out that beautiful light elf is his mate, all bets are off with the killing thing. He'll protect Chelsea with his last breath if necessary. Afterall, she's his.

The surprises don't stop at finding a mate. Someone forgot to tell Zaos he's the son of a dragon and a Dark Elf who are mortal enemies. The drama explodes until the realm is at risk and everyone's life is at stake. But Chelsea isn't one to sit idle and watch. She's about to learn that saving a world can get a girl killed. And it'll destroy Zaos to know there's nothing he can do to stop her.

Published By
Latin Goddess Press
Winter Springs, FL 32708
http://millytaiden.com
Dark King

 Created with Vellum

—For My Readers

Thank you for allowing me to live my dream!

Hope you follow us into the Crystal Kingdom: New Worlds

Chelsea's heartrate barely registered above her normal resting beats, her breathing was the same. And the longer she ran, the calmer her body became. She thought it was funny that it baffled the shit out of her high school and college coaches.

She wasn't sure how her vital signs remained so calm when she pushed her body to the edge. In school and secondary education, she ran long-distance on the track team. That was a miracle worker helping her through her teenage years. When the snobbiest clique picked on her or when a boy she liked ignored her, she went for a run and the solution became evident.

Her grandmother told her to find something

she liked to do and focus all her energy on it to become the best. That advice certainly worked for her half-sister, Avery. She was freaky incredible at playing video games. The girl had even made money playing. If only she were paid to run.

Maybe one day. She was in training for her first full marathon. Sixty miles a week was her goal at this point. The natural high from the rush of endorphins always elevated her mood when feeling lonely, especially now after the most embarrassing breakup of her entire life.

Chelsea always understood her boyfriend of two years was hesitant when it came to spending a lot of money. His family wasn't as well off as hers and he worked for every cent he had. Though she never worried about it, she figured he hadn't asked her to marry him because he couldn't afford a ring.

So when she thought it was time to move their relationship to the next level, she planned on popping the question to him. Boy, was that the biggest mistake of her life.

He'd been a little stressed recently, worried about the stability of his job. Chelsea decided she was going to make him happy again by buying them both engagement rings so he wouldn't have to worry about finding a way to pay for them.

She'd made a date at their favorite bistro and set up ahead of time for the waiters to bring out balloons and start up the mariachi band when he said yes. She was so excited, she couldn't keep the smile off her face the whole day.

When he arrived at the restaurant, he seemed nervous and kept glancing at his watch. She didn't know what was up, but she didn't want to ruin the night, so she kept the conversation light, talking about the things they could do over the weekend.

When they had nearly finished their meals, Chelsea finally asked if everything was okay. He said he had a question and Chelsea said she had one, too, starting to get excited after the strange dinner. He told her to go first. She excused herself to the restroom then searched for the waiter and the band to stand by.

She thought about getting down on one knee, but that wasn't her style. Instead, she stood by the table with the entire dining room looking on and took his hand in hers and laid it over her heart.

"Dylan, you are the love of my life. We were friends for the longest time who grew to care more for each other. I want the entire world to know how much I love you." The waiter stepped up and presented a tray with origami-folded napkins that had their rings displayed. "Will you marry me, Dylan?"

He stared at her with terror in his eyes. It was cute and a little funny how off guard she caught him. The mariachi trio started in before he answered.

But when he didn't break into a smile, and his ex-girlfriend walked up behind him and laid a hand on his shoulder, her insides twisted.

Dylan opened his mouth. "Uh," then the chickenshit looked up at his ex. The woman rolled her eyes.

"What he wants to tell you," the bitch hollered over the band, "is that we're getting back together."

Chelsea's world zoomed down to Dylan's red face. How long had they been planning this? How long had they been sleeping together before now?

Now she understood why he always wanted to come to her place and seldom went to his. What had he been hiding all this time?

Chelsea dropped his hand and stared at him. "Two years? It took you two years to figure out you wanted to go back to the bitch who bossed you around and told you to suck her toes or she wouldn't suck your dick?'"

Yeah, when Dylan told her that story, Chelsea nearly fell over laughing. That was one reason he broke up with the *bitch*. With that public reveal, the girlfriend scowled at him. Whatever. Chelsea didn't care.

She grabbed the ring display and her purse and walked out while the Mexican music blared behind her. Let the bastard pay for the meal.

That was the last time she ate there. And hadn't seen Dylan since. To this day, she didn't understand why it took so long for him to let her in on his secret. Had she acted too quickly concerning their relationship? Was she not observant enough to catch the signs? Was he ever really into her?

One thing was for certain, she'd never let that happen to her again. If the guy didn't try to win her over, then she wasn't giving him a second look. Could be why she was approaching the big three-O and not had a date in six months. Her heart pinged with the thought.

The transition back to a single existence was hard after a couple years of always having someone at her side. Always cooking for someone else. Always cleaning up after somebody.

At the stoplight, jogging in place, Chelsea thought about her sister who had the perfect love connection. Even though they had different fathers, they were a lot alike in personality. Their grandmother kept them in check when it came to being grounded and having common sense, not letting the girls' trust fund accounts be taken for granted.

But what the hell did money mean to a friggin' fairy princess?

Well, Grandmom was more of an elf princess. But whatever. Learning that explained a lot in her own life. Why her ears were tilted at a weird angle and sort of pointy, but not as much as her sister's. Her favorite movie was the *Lord of the Rings*, as was Avery's. She could spend hours in her grandmother's special room where she collected everything elven. Even growing up, Chelsea's Halloween costumes had always been a species of elves.

And she was so jealous—in a loving way— that her sister was matched up with an elf king. A freaking king, not to mention he was from another dimension or plane or something like that. She hadn't quite understood all that when Grandmom told them about the Crystal Kingdom a few months ago.

She missed her sister. They hadn't been as close as she wanted since she lived with her father. When her mom remarried and Avery was born, Chelsea was starting grade school, making new friends and figuring out how to navigate a scary world. A baby sister wasn't always at the top of the list for things to see.

Crossing the lanes of traffic with a few others awake at this early hour, she wondered if there was a way to see her sister, now that the girl was in the Twilight Zone. Avery's birthday was coming up and it would be cool to have a surprise party or maybe just surprise guests intruding on her bliss.

She bounced up the steps to her building's front entrance and stepped inside. She cooled down with a brisk walk to the mailboxes, then up the stairs to her floor. When she opened her apartment door, she heard her phone ringing.

Dread filled her. Calls like this carried bad news. Something happened during the night and now her life would be void of someone she loved, or something would change in the least.

CHAPTER TWO

Chelsea stared at the portable phone charging on its base in her kitchen. Dust covered it enough that she swiped a finger across the handset, leaving a well-defined trail. She lifted it and answered with a shaky hello.

"Good morning, Chelsea. This is your grandmom calling. Don't worry, I don't have bad news. In fact, it's quite good, hopefully."

She blew out a breath and fell onto a breakfast settee chair. "Grandmom," she replied, "you scared the crap out of me."

"Sorry, dear, but I knew you'd be up."

And her elder just happened to call the second she stepped through her apartment door? Right. Grandmom didn't have magical powers. No, not at all. Chelsea rolled her eyes. Those in the family who thought the older woman was suffering dementia were off their own rockers. Grandmom was the real thing.

"I had a thought," her grandmother said. "You know Avery's birthday is coming up and I thought it would be nice for you and a few of the cousins to pop in and visit."

Pop in? Just pop into a different dimension? Sure.

"That would be a great idea, Grandmom." Not that she hadn't thought that herself five minutes ago. The woman was scary magical. Elf princess? More like read-your-mind-teleport-to-the-impossible-conjure-up-anything elf witch princess. But Chelsea couldn't love anyone more.

"When were you thinking?" she asked. She could take a couple days off work next week. When one went to a magical place, you stayed longer than a few hours, right? What was the point of going if there wasn't enough time to see all the sights? Did an elven forest even have sights? How different could a tree be? It's not like it moved on its own or anything.

"I thought maybe this afternoon you could corral your cousins and come over."

Well, thanks for the advance warning, Grandmom. Good thing it's Saturday. "Okay. I can do that, I guess. I don't have any errands to run today."

"Wonderful," the elder said. "Be sure to wear your running shoes, and dress comfortably in sturdy clothes. See you soon." With that, she hung up.

Sturdy clothes? What the hell? Chelsea laid the handset back onto the base. Grandmom was up to something. The woman was horrible at keeping secrets. But what could it be? Maybe it was just the surprise for Avery she was excited about.

After a shower and breakfast, it was still too early on a Saturday to call her cousins. She'd learned long ago to not call anyone before eight in the morning on the weekends. Which meant she got most of her stuff done before making contact with the outside world. And a lot of the time that included work she'd brought home.

Being a divorce mediator meant she took a lot of time studying the divorce case and issues that brought about the problems that seemed unfixable. A lot of times, being creative was the only way to find solutions. Some of the things she thought of could only come from the mind of a demented human—like cutting off his balls, slice by slice. She didn't share those, of course.

Several hours later, a little after one in the afternoon, Chelsea met up with her three cousins at Grandmom's home. Wren, Daphne, and Lilah were the ones always going to all the family functions, keeping the peace, and making sure gossip didn't split the family apart. Without their efforts, Chelsea wasn't sure where the clan would be. Probably not talking to each other, if not in prison for killing each other.

After hugs were exchanged, Grandmom sat them on the sofa and turned serious. "Now, ladies," she started, "you are going to a place where they think humans are make-believe and are horrible creatures by how we've taken care of our planet."

Chelsea understood what her grandmother meant. Humans' history of destroying the earth was well known by everyone who lived on the globe. Why not other places, too?

"So," Grandmom continued, "keep to yourselves who you are. Each of you have a touch of fae blood, but elf blood runs true through your veins with human blood. If someone asks, tell them you are guests of the elf king. They should leave you alone if they mean you harm."

Lilah sat straighter and looked at the others. "Others will want to hurt us?" Growing up, she'd always been the one to second guess whatever antic the other kids were up to. She'd watch while others fell and broke bones or jumped the fence and got chased by dogs or paddled for wrongdoing. She claimed to be allergic to getting hurt.

"No, of course, not," Grandmom said. "But you know as well as I that there is usually someone who is the bad apple."

Couldn't disagree with that.

"Now, are you ladies ready to go?"

Chelsea's insides churned. They were really crossing into another dimension where goblins—gobalus—and fairies were real. Holy shit, she couldn't believe it. Hearing about it was one thing, seeing it was another.

Grandmom opened a small box on the sofa table beside her. From it, she pulled out three pieces of cloth with something wrapped inside each. "Since Avery and her friends are living in Crystal Kingdom full-time, the fairy queen has created several sets of portal stones so more of us can travel back and forth." She kept a stone then handed one to Chelsea and another of the ladies.

"When all three gems touch, a passageway into the kingdom will open." Grandmom stood. "Ready?" She held out her palm with the stone and Chelsea and Daphne touched theirs to hers. With a light hum, a round section of air in the middle of the room changed to show a village among trees with people milling about.

"Quickly, now, everyone through." Grandmom waved them toward the distortion floating in space. Before Chelsea stepped over, her grandmother handed her the third stone. "Take care of them, granddaughter. I trust you more with magic since you have some inside you." Grandmom gestured for her to step over which Chelsea did. "Have fun. Tell Avery I said happy birthday and that I love her."

"I will, Grandmom." Chelsea was about to turn when she heard the elder woman's voice again.

"Oh, Chelsea, be sure to hold one of the stones when you come back."

"Okay." She could barely hear her grandmother now that she was on the other side. She pocketed the stones and the portal closed.

CHAPTER THREE

Her grandmother and the living room disappeared as the portal closed and Chelsea stared at the forest that wasn't of her world, but easily could've been. Tall trees like those in California she'd seen in photos scattered about.

This area of the village had large open spaces where people worked or gathered. The ground was soft with pine needles she could probably walk barefoot on. A sweet perfume-like scent floated on the air. Breathing it in revitalized her spirit, giving her more pep. She bet Grandmom loved living here. And thinking of the elder...

Had her grandmother just said that she, Chelsea, the older sister, had magic in her? Like real, honest-to-God magic? Why hadn't she told her before now? How did she use it? What did it do? Oh my freakin' god. She could do magic!

A squeal behind her turned her around to see Avery squeezing her cousins. Chelsea hurried to catch up. "Happy early birthday," she said.

Avery gushed, wiping away a tear. Chelsea hadn't thought about her sister being homesick. How could she when she was in a place as beautiful and serene like this? And married to something that looked like that.

Tylen, Avery's elf husband, walked toward them with a wide smile on his face. Lordy. Could a man look any more delicious? Really, he needed to put a shirt on before her tongue fell out. She averted her eyes and mentally kicked herself. That was her brother-in-law, for goodness' sake.

"I miss you," she told Avery. "Can't you guys live on Earth?" Tears touched her eyes. She hadn't realized how lonely she was until this second.

Avery laughed. "I don't think Tylen would do well in our world. He would want to make everything better and put humanity back in the Stone Age."

Chelsea snorted. "That can't be any worse than it is now."

Tylen wrapped an arm around Avery. "I heard that, woman. And yes, I'd want to make everything better. But that would take magic the likes of which I don't have."

"Yeah," Daphne said, "it's a magic called politics. And you don't want to get involved unless you're a glutton for punishment."

Tylen smiled. "A glutton for punishment, I am not. But a glutton for other things, perhaps." His eyes locked onto her sister's and Chelsea felt the love and lust between the two. She wondered how long until she was an aunt? Judging by this, not long.

"Okay, sis," Chelsea said, "remember we're here before you two start shucking the clothes."

Avery giggled, placing a hand on the man's, um, elf's chest. "You guys, this is Tylen, my husband, and by the way, he's the king." He rolled his eyes as Avery belly laughed.

Wren leaned forward to Chelsea's ear. "Did I miss something?"

Chelsea shook her head. "Nah, Avery lives in her own world and they all like her there."

Her sister cleared her throat. "Sorry guys.

17

Inside joke." She turned to the sex on a stick. "Tylen, this is my half-sister sisters Chelsea and Daphne, Wren and Lilah are our cousins." Each of the girls waved when their name was called

Chelsea put her hand out to shake. "Nice to meet you."

Tylen stared at the hand then looked to Avery. "You did this also when we met. What does it mean?"

Avery reached over and shook her sister's hand. "It's called a handshake. That's how we greet each other if a hug isn't acceptable."

Tylen held his hand out and Chelsea took it. He said, "Nice to meet you." He properly met the cousins, and Chelsea almost died as all three swooned when he touched and smiled at them. She'd had to agree that his smile could set under-wear on fire. And then drench them from being wet.

"Go play with the men and behave." At his return smile, Chelsea heard her three cousins sigh. Wouldn't it be nice to have a man like that? Yowzer.

Avery gathered the foursome and led them toward a group of people standing at worktables.

Women and men loaded baskets of food onto the tables for others to prepare to eat.

Chelsea asked, "Do you guys spend all day making food, since you don't have refrigerators and stuff?"

Avery raised a brow at her. "Really, Chel? We might not have electricity, but we have magic." Her sister twirled her hand and a vine on a nearby tree waved at them.

"Did you do that?" Wren asked, her jaw dropping open. "What else can you do?"

Avery sighed. "That's all I can do. My magic is different than others."

"What do you mean?" Lilah asked. Chelsea would like to know that answer also. Would her magic be like her sister's?

"I'm what they call a bowl of nature or something," Avery answered.

"And that means..." Chelsea asked.

Avery smiled. "It means my magic makes other's magic a lot stronger. I'm a bowl of power ready to be tapped."

Behind Chelsea, Lilah whispered, "Yeah, I know who would like to *tap* into that bowl." They all laughed as Avery turned bright red.

"Hey," Avery said with a smile, "I'm married,

so tapping, or in my case pounding, is legal."

The girls screamed with laughter. Her cousins were a riotous group when they got together. At family reunions, she felt sorry for the men they'd married. No telling what words would pop out of someone's mouth.

"Okay, guys," Avery said, "ladies here don't talk that way, unless they're one of the elders who don't care how the truth affects someone. They can be brutal. No one is safe from embarrassment from them. I love them to death."

They arrived at the tables, and Chelsea watched the action running like a smooth assembly line. Carts brought in baskets from the forest, loaded with foodstuff, and were placed on the end of a table.

From there, the baskets were taken to other tables for washing and reloading into smaller weaved containers. There was such a variety, Chelsea wondered how they got the food.

She asked, "Do you use magic to conjure food?"

Her sister whipped around with her hand covering her mouth, eyes wide.

"What?" Chelsea said, glancing around to see if anyone else had the same reaction.

Her sister twisted, searching for someone. "I don't know where Ry is. So I'll tell you before she overhears you." Avery straightened, stretched her neck, and lifted her chin. "And I quote, it is not honorable to use the magic gifted to us by the Powers for needs we can tend to ourselves."

Chelsea looked to the girls, her brows scrunched. Wren mouthed, "That was a whole lotta nope in my dictionary." The others nodded.

Avery huffed. "It means magic is only used for certain things, and something as simple as growing our own food doesn't need magic. That's not being honorable or something."

Chelsea and the ladies stood staring.

"Never mind," Avery said. "We can talk while help—"

A man similar in stature to Tylen ran out of the forest into the village. "Fire water! We need fire water now."

With that, the neatly assembled lines exploded into a mass of bodies rushing here and there.

"Oh my god," Avery said and ran toward the man. Chelsea followed. As she got closer, she saw the man was carrying an unconscious child. "What happened?" Avery brushed the sweat off the child's forehead.

He said, "She has a misthistle thorn in her leg, Your Highness."

Avery's face scrunched. "Please call me Avery. I am a simple elf just like everyone else." Chelsea was surprised, twice. First when he called her sister Your Highness. Grandmom said Avery was mated to the king of the elves, but hearing that title attached to Avery sounded very weird. In no way was her sister a princess or queen. All she wore at home were old jeans and scraggly T-shirts.

Then when Avery rejected the honorific, Chelsea was a bit taken aback. The girl was married to the king. Yet, she considered herself the same as the villagers. Yes, that would've been Avery. Chelsea was proud of her. But the tears in her sis's eyes worried her.

"What's misthistle?" Chelsea asked.

The man glanced up at her. "It is an extremely poisonous plant. Just touching it can kill you."

Avery looked as surprised as Chelsea felt. Her sister mumbled, "No, please, no." Avery laid her hand on the child's flushed face. "Don't you die, Peatra. We just found your power. Now we have to practice more. You can't leave, little one."

CHAPTER FOUR

"**P**ut that boulder there." Zaos pointed to a low spot in the pile of rock they were building up to support the ceiling of the cave. If those damn dragons would keep to their own fucking land, he wouldn't have to do this so often.

The cave-ins were becoming more severe in this section of the underground hollows. The nursery was to be moved next so it was even farther from the rear of the caverns. They couldn't lose what little future they had.

Using magic, the dark elf with the large rock floated the stone to the top of the stack, wedging it tightly.

"That will do for now." Zaos turned to the

line of elves with their own rocks. "Set your stones in front of the wall and return to your duties. I will need some of you when the females are ready to relocate the infants in a sun cycle. I will contact you."

He turned his back to them and strode toward the throne room. King Gorwin commanded Zaos to update him on the status of the rock integrity. It was the same as it always was—too demon's hell weak and getting weaker. They had to do something with the dragons. He didn't want to go to war again. But this was his home and he would fight to the death to protect it.

He entered the ostentatious room, not even noticing the gold embellishments on the walls and columns or the fancy plush rugs with mounds of unused pillows. The extravagant paintings on the wall meant nothing to him though the king sat for hours staring at them. There weren't even elves in the artwork. What did the king see in them?

Zaos quickly reached the flamboyant golden throne where King Gorwin parked his ass all day. It was no wonder the man was the size of a small dragon. He ate continuously and seldom moved. The food would've been better if distributed to the children. They were all too thin in his opinion.

But who was he to say anything but another minion of the dark king?

He lowered to a knee and bowed his head. "Your Highness, the ceilings have been refortified but dust falls to the cave floor in many other places. We must deal with the dragons again."

"I am the ruler here, Zaos. Not you. Do not tell me how to run my kingdom," the king said calmly then eased back on the magic.

"Yes, Your Highness." Too bad he couldn't tell the dumb-shit leader that he ruled a bunch of fucking holes in the ground that amounted to nothing. They didn't even see the sun unless they went outside. No wonder their species was dying off little by little.

Life hadn't always been this bad. Long ago when he was a youngling, though it was now a distant memory, he barely remembered playing in the sun with many others his age. The forest had been teeming with life and beauty. They'd chased bugs and practiced imitating the bird calls.

In the time after midday meal, he and others would lie among the fire lilies and watch the deep green leaves sway in the breeze.

But that was so long ago, he sometimes wondered if those memories were only dreams.

Fantasies concocted by a mind desperate for a reason to continue after so many centuries.

The king stood from his gaudy seat and shuffled toward the side wall. Extending his hand over the rock floor, the king's magic caused green stalks to shoot up and blossom into seedlings then continue to full growth ready to eat.

A good variety filled the dry dirt. Gourds, roots, jeves, and pomeracs. But the quality had lacked in the past summers. When the king was younger and his power not waning, food was plentiful. It seemed like all of the elves' powers were diminishing. Even his own.

He wondered if that meant the end was coming for his people. Without magic, there was no food, no water, no weapons, no anything. Everything they had came from magic. He wouldn't doubt that the magic was becoming depleted. Was there only so much available from the Powers? Could they run out?

The king sighed, exhaustion in his stance. "Call the males to meal. Make sure the females get their share. We do not want to lose the few remaining."

After everyone had filled their dish, including the females, Zaos gathered the little that remained for himself. He sat with a group of guards who patrolled the area leading to the entrance.

"What do you think?" Tel, one of the elves he didn't care for, leaned on the table whispering to those across from him.

"Think of what?" Zaos asked.

Tel jumped from Zaos's sudden appearance. Tel sat and said nothing, instead picking at his plate of food.

Zaos glanced at the others to see if one of them would answer. They stared at him, wide-eyed and not moving.

"What?" he said? He turned to Darfin who he knew would tell him what was going on. The elf couldn't keep a secret even if you didn't tell it to him. "Darfin," he said. The elf snapped his head up and his eyes got as big as his plate.

"Y-yes, milord?" The poor elf's hands shook. Zaos hated to make the guy the center of attention. If Darfin told him though, then the others would never say anything around him again. That wasn't what he wanted. Dragon shit.

"Tell me, Darfin, what is it about me that would keep you from telling me something?"

The elf's face scrunched up. "Milord?"

Zaos raised a hand to halt the answer. "Let's

try this another way. What makes me different from all of you at this table?" His eyes went from one elf to another. Of course, Tel displayed a scowl.

"You are too nice," one of them replied.

Zaos erupted into laughter. "Are you serious? You treat me differently because I'm too nice?" For being a dark elf, being nice was not a compliment. Nice would get you killed. Nice meant weakness, and in this place of survival of the strongest, the weak didn't last long.

But that rule didn't apply to him. He was the biggest of anyone there. Weakness was not in his personality.

Zaos knew why he was different from the others, but thanks to his magic, no one but his parents knew his secret.

"Milord," Darfin said, "you have the king's ear." Yes, he was the unspoken next in command, but why did that matter?

"You're the king's fuck boy is more the truth," Tel mumbled.

Zaos heard the comment, as did the others nearby if their gasps gave any hint. Again, everyone's eyes widened and turned to him. He swallowed his anger. His strength and magic could easily kill any of these dwarf shits. But to display that would bring ruination to him.

"Luckily for you, Tel, I am too nice or I would challenge you to the death right now." More gasps echoed around the table. Tel's face flushed, but he said nothing. Zaos waited to see if the elf would call his bluff. Everyone remained silent and continued eating.

The tension drifted away as the elves finished eating, magicking away their dirty dishes, then leaving. But the idea that Tel had something bad planned ate at him. He never liked nor trusted the guard.

Leaving the meal area, he searched out one of the men who was at the table. He would have his answer one way or another.

Just inside the cave's opening, one of the guards stood. He would do. Zaos stopped next to him. "What was Tel saying that he wanted everyone's thoughts on?"

The guard blanched. "I-I do not approve of his idea, milord. I will have no part in it."

That wasn't the answer he wanted. "You will have no part of what?"

The guard stepped back, bowing his head. "He wants to take several females from the light elves and pass them around until they are all impregnated. He believes this will bring back the place of power we once had."

It took only a second for Zaos's shock to burn into rage. He stepped outside the entrance, hands in fists, and a ground-shaking roar thrust from his chest into the air, scaring away birds. At that moment, he was a force of nature that not even the wind wanted to fuck with.

CHAPTER FIVE

\

Chelsea stood spellbound witnessing her sister cry over a little girl who looked to be straight from heaven. If the child was moments from death, she didn't look it.

Movement to the side caught Chelsea's attention. A woman was running toward them with something in her hand.

Avery nearly screamed, "Ry, you have to save her, please."

"Hush, My Queen, she will be fine," the woman said. "Hold her head up," she instructed. Avery was in no shape to be doing anything that required stable hands. So, she stepped forward and lifted the little one's head.

Chelsea nearly gasped at the child's angel-like

appearance. She was beautiful with a smooth, flawless, pale complexion. Her blonde hair had golden highlights that would cost big time at any hair salon on Earth.

The woman tilted the container, which looked more like a leather canteen, for water to fall past the small, bow-shaped lips. "Drink, Peatra. You must drink."

Chelsea noticed something mixed in with the water. It looked like pieces of yellow and orange flowers chopped down. The man had called for fire water. So where was the fire?

"Where is the thorn?" the woman asked. The man nodded toward the girl's legs. There on her calf, a scary boil-type chunk of skin appeared gangrene. What frightened Chelsea was how quickly the black sickness spread through her leg. It crept out like vein-thin snakes from the center.

The water lady laid her finger next to the open soar, and Chelsea couldn't believe her eyes when the thorn wiggled its way out with no one touching it. It fell onto the woman's palm then a man carefully plucked it up and walked away.

Twisting the leg so the injury faced up, the elf poured water directly onto the sore. The second the liquid touched, a small flame ignited as if burning the spot. Then the flames seemed to be sucked into the hole of the skin. Chelsea's mouth gaped as the black poison spreading in the child's veins disappeared as if the fire was eating it. When all the toxin was gone, the sore once again burst into a flame, then quickly dwindled, leaving the skin *unmarred*.

The girl shivered in the man's arms as he passed her to Avery. Avery hugged the child to her. "You're going to be okay, baby. The water cured you."

The small eyes opened to a brilliant hue. Her weak smile showed off her white baby teeth.

The water woman sighed. "Take her home. Her parents have been told of the situation and are probably waiting for you. Tell them she will be fine, but needs bed rest and lots of water to rehydrate what the fire took out."

Chelsea stepped back, nearly bumping into Avery as her sister went to follow. "I have to make sure she's okay." The pleading tears in Avery's eyes nearly broke Chelsea's heart. Her hand rested on her chest as if to stop the pain.

"Go on, sis," she hollered, "we got this." They watched silently as the three hurried through the trees.

"We do?" Daphne whispered. "Who's got this, because I don't got this."

"I've haven't gotten it in months," Wren added.

"Me neither," Chelsea commented.

"What's fire water?" Lilah asked. "Will it get rid of my spider veins?" Both Daphne and Wren elbowed her. "What?" she said. "How am I going to attract a guy with these ugly things?" The others choose to ignore her at the moment.

The woman with the fire water turned to them, her brow raised higher than Chelsea had ever seen. "Greetings, guests. I am Ryllea, one of the elders of the village. I assume you are friends of our queen."

They nodded, no one daring to speak as the words of welcome sounded like the four were being scolded. "Come children. The breakfast meal will be ready shortly." They all looked and each other and shrugged, then jogged to catch up with the elder who looked twenty-something.

Ryllea gathered them around a table and put a basket of long purple things resembling green beans in the middle. She grabbed a handful and snapped one into three pieces. She continued snapping without saying a word.

Chelsea glanced at the others, grabbed several violet beans, and did as Ryllea did. The others followed suit.

Without looking up, the elder said, "Fire water has the strongest healing power in nature. Since misthistle is one of the deadliest plants, only fire water can save the unfortunate elf. Of course, if Peatra had strong blood magic, it is possible she could heal herself, but she is only a baby."

Chelsea grabbed another handful of lavender things. "I noticed something in the water the little girl drank. What was it?"

"That is the ground up pieces of a fire lily. It is what gives the water the healing abilities."

"Never heard of a fire lily," Wren said.

"Well, duh," Daphne replied. "We're not on Earth, dipshit."

Wren slapped her arm with the back of her hand. "Hey, be nice or I'll put you in my next story and kill you off painfully."

"Are we finished?" Ryllea asked.

The girls lowered their heads with apologies of sorry mumbled.

"The fire lily came about many millennia ago. When the dark elves and dragons were at their height in battle, a dark elf slipped into the dragons' land and killed the pregnant queen. She was deeply loved by all creatures in this dimension for she would sacrifice her wellbeing to get to the sick. She was a powerful healer. The strongest that had ever been.

"The peoples fell into sadness and the world's heart weighed heavily. The plants refused to share their foods and the waters dried up. Even the skies were despondent as they cried for many sun cycles creating deadly currents in the valleys.

"When the time came, the dragon king buried his love in the fields of the sunrise. Many visited her place of rest to thank her for curing someone they loved or to show her their true hearts."

"According to legend passed through the ages, the field in which she lay started growing a beautiful flower with ribbon-like tendrils, that when fluttering in the breeze together, looked like the flame of a fire. That flower, named the fire lily, was a highly magical plant that healed almost anything, just like the powerful queen could."

"They sound beautiful," Wren commented. "Do they grow nearby?"

"No," Ryllea said. "Only in the lands of the dark elves and dragons."

Lilah squealed. "Are there really dragons here? Can we see one?"

Chelsea could only shake her head. "I thought I brought my *adult* cousins, but instead I got the five-year-olds."

Daphne threw a bean at her. "Come on, Chel. We're talking real dragons here. Not some bozo in a purple dragon costume who loves everyone."

"Hey," Wren cut in, "I happened to like Barney when I was little."

"Ugh, you would." Lilah rolled her eyes.

When they were finally quiet, Ryllea continued. "Dragons and dark elves live quite a distance from here."

"Of course." Lilah agreed like she had any clue what the elder was talking about. Chelsea frowned at her, silently telling her to be quiet. "Why are they called dark elves? Do they look different?"

"That is another story entirely," Ryllea answered. "Let it be said that since they live underground close to the dead lands, 'dark' fits their personas quite well." She grabbed her basket of snipped beans. "Bring your holders, children, and come with me. It is time to eat."

CHAPTER SIX

J ust having learned there were real dragons in this dimension along with dark elves, Chelsea felt a little discombobulated. She knew she was on a different planet, but telling her brain all the stuff she'd known as make-believe actually existed was surreal.

Chelsea and the others followed Ryllea at a short distance.

"Why does Ryllea keep calling us children?" Lilah asked.

"Really?" Daphne said, "after your dumb dragon comment, you have to ask?"

Chelsea answered, "Grandmom told us some of the elves were thousands of years old."

"Holy shit? Thousands?" Daphne said. "And she called herself an elder."

"I bet she was around when the first fire lily bloomed," Wren whispered.

"Shush," Chelsea said, glancing around. "They have supersonic ears. Everyone can hear you."

More of the others had gathered the closer they got to a place where tables were set up but there were no chairs.

"We're not going to stand the entire time we eat, are we?" Daphne whispered.

"I don't know," Chelsea replied.

Lilah turned and walked backward a few steps then pivoted around. "I don't see anyone bring chairs, just more gorgeous men who really need me to touch them. I mean, really, to be an elf, do you have to be absolutely stunning."

"That knocks you out of being an elf, Lilah." Daphne smiled at her.

Lilah stuck her tongue out at her cousin. "Shut it, girl. I'm not the one who has a scar on her forehead from walking in shoes too high and doing a face plant in front of everyone."

All the girls but Daphne laughed. Chelsea heard about the story, but wasn't a witness to the scene she sure was embarrassing as hell. What would the family be like without the three of them? Quiet. Maybe peaceful. Nah, she wouldn't want it any other way.

As others gathered to the tables, the girls saw where the chairs came from—the ground, as roots popped out and formed seating customized to the person—elf—sitting. They all stood with mouths gaping. She was sure they looked stupid in front of all the hot men.

She didn't think they would ever get used to magic. It was so different.

"This way young ones." Ryllea's voice carried to them. She was at the front waving to them. Another woman, beautiful beyond words, was seated at the table where their babysitter stood. The elven woman looked way more like a queen than her sister ever would.

Making her way through the crowd, Chelsea looked around for Avery. Where was she? Why was that little girl so important to her sister? She hoped the child was okay. One thing she noticed was how many children there were. Scores of them. She hadn't seen them before. They must've been somewhere else while the adults prepared food.

As more joined, she realized how large the village was. They must've been spread out doing chores because this was double the amount that helped fix the meal. How many more were there? The quantity of food now made sense.

The four ladies gathered at the table like they had seen others do and waited for their chairs to form. Chelsea almost laughed and clapped her hands at how exciting this all was. Magic. Wow!

When they were seated, the elf woman smiled at them. "Welcome to our home. My name is Velatha." She bowed her head slightly. *Definitely majestic*, Chelsea thought. "We are happy to meet you, friends of our queen."

"Uh..." Chelsea looked at her cousins to see if they were going to say anything. They seemed to only speak when they weren't supposed to. "Thank you. We are happy to be here." That was rather lame, but she wasn't prepared to have a conversation with a complete stranger.

Velatha looked directly at her. "I am to tell you that the queen will return as soon as she is certain Peatra will live."

"The child is darling," Chelsea said. "My sister seems to care for her a lot. Is that normal?"

The elven woman smiled. "Your sister is a

very special elf. Her heart runs deep, able to hold much love for everyone. That is why she is a natura patera."

The cousins jerked their heads toward the woman. Lilah gasped. "Is that like cancer? Will she be all right?"

Velatha's brows scrunched down. "I do not know what cancer is."

Chelsea waved off the question. "Never mind, that. What does natura patera mean in your language?"

"Our queen is a carrier of power that helps other magical creatures become much stronger in body and magic. Without her, we never would have destroyed Xubus. We would all be slaves to him. We will love her always for her sacrifice."

"Whoa," Chelsea said, "what sacrifice? That doesn't sound good."

Vel smiled. "She was willing to give her soul for ours. She risked her life trying to free us. Xubus would have killed her if he'd known what she had planned. Then our queen nearly drained herself completely when sending power to her elves when it came time to fight. Of course, she didn't know what she was doing with the crown, but she has learned to control it now."

The foursome sat astounded. Grandmom hadn't mentioned anything about all that. What else had she not told them? Chelsea had no idea who this sister of hers was. It was as if she'd grown into a real leader in a matter of weeks. Again, pride flowed through her for what her little sister had become. A true queen.

"So, about the girl," Chelsea said, returning to the original conversation.

"Yes." Vel paused, staring down at the table. "Peatra had a difficult birth. She came too early and was not ready to live outside her mother's womb. But with help from our healers and fire water, the girl has grown into her own. But she has..." Vel looked away again then turned back, "challenges most younglings don't go through. Your sister, our queen, was able to help Peatra find her magic."

Chelsea asked, "What does that mean? *Find* her magic?"

"Magic comes from the heart. It is not evil, nor is it good. It just is. What the wielder of the magic intends with its power decides if it is to be used to harm others or help them. Peatra had yet to discover how to access her abilities.

"Our queen shared her magic with the child,

opening in the little one the path to her own heart." Vel smiled and leaned forward as if to share a secret. The four girls mimicked her, all leaning in together. No, they weren't obviously gossiping. But Chelsea was too entranced with the storyteller to worry about others.

"The event was quite endearing. I do not believe your sister had any idea of what she was doing when she helped Peatra. But now, the girl is the most powerful among all the younglings." The elf bowed her head. "Perhaps that may be enough to save her life from the misthistle. I'm sure our queen will do everything she can to boost the healing abilities."

Wren huffed. "This completely blows my mind."

Velatha looked at her frightened eyes. "Do you need a healer?" She was nearly out of her chair before Chelsea laid a hand on her arm.

"No. It's just a saying. She is fine." Chelsea glared at Wren. "Be mindful of what y'all say." Visiting could be a total disaster if the gap in the language barrier wasn't watched. She could see one of her cousins flying off the handle and telling an elf to kiss her ass. That would so not be good.

"Sorry," Wren said. "But how is Avery so powerful here? She never showed signs of magic at home, did she?"

That was a great question. Chelsea thought back through the years when she and her sister were together. Being five years older and living with her father, and not their mother, she hadn't been around Avery much when they were young except for holidays when Mom picked her up.

But no one mentioned anything about objects floating through the air or mysterious happenings of any kind. Grandmom sure hadn't let out any clues about being—wait, maybe she had dropped hints on how to use magic, but in a roundabout way. Telling her to focus on what she loved to do and become the best. Could magic affect her running?

The crowd quieted as everyone had taken a seat. At the long table in front of them, Tylen stood and silence floated in the air. All around her, Chelsea heard the sounds of nature. Being a city girl, she didn't know what creatures made those chirps, tweets, and buzzing, but they felt comforting, calming.

She took in a deep breath, smelling the fresh scents of a forest with clean air, and food. She almost wanted to stay a while, to remain in such a paradise. But she had a job and responsibilities at home.

Tylen welcomed everyone to the meal and mentioned what had happened to the little girl and that the queen was with the child. So much for visiting her sister. That really bummed her. She wanted to spend time with her sister. Chelsea needed her in more ways than one.

CHAPTER SEVEN

Zaos could rip heads off and tear limbs from bodies, he was so angry. And that was exactly what Tel deserved for his plan to take female elves against their will and force them to have children.

Standing outside the entrance to the cave, he had to think where Tel would be working this shift. From the trees, he heard someone say, "Tel is in the training field." Obviously, the fucker wasn't working but waiting for Zaos to fight. *Bring it on, fucker.*

He marched to the one area where the forest didn't penetrate the land. This field they used for gatherings and practices. The only thing Zaos didn't like was that it bordered the dead land.

That alone was almost enough to make the area unsafe, but his men knew to stay away from it.

Here the elves trained with weapons and sparred. Since they had little magic, none was ever performed or depended upon in battle. Train with the sword, death by the sword.

All around him, his sensitive ears picked up leaves being thrashed as elves ran to watch the spectacle and told others. More than likely, the entire clan would witness firsthand his wrath. There was no mistake why he was second to their king. He was stronger, taller, smarter than the others. He was almost an anomaly, a throwback to the time before the dark elves fell from grace.

Passing the tree line, Zaos saw Tel standing in the clearing, sword already in hand. Seemed the bastard had this set up. Did he not know who he was fighting? Did he think he could take Zaos? The elf wasn't stupid. Which meant something else was in the works.

Zaos's cool head prevailed as the path through the trees calmed his roiling mind and heart. Tel would still die, just not as quickly or violently.

When he approached, Tel smiled. First time for everything. "Well, now, Zaos. Seems something has you upset. Whatever could it be?"

"Can it, asshole," he said.

Tel's brows drew down. "You've had the strangest dialog since your return. I wonder where you truly went, because it wasn't to the gobalus as you claim."

The answer to that question would never flow from his tongue. The witch with long black hair and a white stripe had her reasons for taking him away.

"I'm here Tel, to let you know your plan to steal females will not happen. If you want to get your rocks off then find another way that doesn't harm innocents."

Tel's brow rose and his head tilted. "Get my rocks off? Very crude, Zaos. I'm surprised you can say such harsh things since you're so *nice*."

He snorted. "There's a lot you don't know about me. Bastards like you give the dark elves an evil image to others. Hurt and kill is all you want to do."

"You forgot fucking, Zaos. I like to fuck females. And I intend to get as much as I want when I want."

"And I told you it wasn't going to happen," Zaos spit out.

"Seems we have a disagreement we need to settle."

"So be it."

Tel lifted his sword to strike Zaos while he was unarmed. With a twist of his wrist, his sword appeared. Tel's eyes narrowed and his swing stopped midair.

"How did you get your sword up so quickly? None of us have that kind of power anymore."

Dwarf shit. He hadn't meant to conjure so quickly. His anger was making him careless.

Tel spit on the ground. "Fight or die." Tel rushed him, Zaos swiping the opposing blade aside, grabbing the smaller elf's shoulder and pushing him to the ground.

"You best remain there if you care to see tomorrow." Zaos stepped back to keep a wide view of the space. No surprises. "What gives you the right to control another person? You are not higher or mightier than anyone else."

"I am owed this." Tel jabbed his sword forward while on the ground, Zaos sideswiping it easily as he burst into laughter.

"How can you possibly think you are owed something by this world?" Zaos asked. "What good have you done to help anyone or thing?"

Tel sprang to his feet, swinging his sword side to side and from over the top. Metal clanged and screeched, grunts from each lost in the wind. Each blow Zaos countered with a block, Tel pushing him back farther and farther. Closer to the dead land. Zaos went on the attack, not letting himself fall into a hairball scheme which included his body touching the dirt. That would be a terrible way to die.

He ignored the spectators cheering them on, though he knew they were there. Warfare had been in their lives for so long, they knew little else. If only the damnation dragons would stop destroying the elves' home, then maybe time could be spent looking for mates. As it was, only the older generations had mates, found when their kind had been numerous.

Zaos studied his opponent's body movements carefully. Tel was tiring, as was he. Adrenaline would only carry a fighter so far with no fear of dying spurring them on. During sparring, he pretended to weaken with the rest as they volleyed strikes. He'd done it for so long that it came second nature to him now.

Once again, Zaos found that Tel drove him toward the edge of the clearing but closer to the trees this time. He didn't like that. His magic urged him to move away. His magic told him to be done with this.

He agreed. This was a stupid waste of time. Fighting each other was useless when there were more important things to do. Zaos called on his inner strength and quickened his blows. Tel's eyes widened as Zaos poured on stamina and power. Just enough so only his opponent would notice.

Zaos swung fast and hard, shattering Tel's weapon and sending the bastard to the ground. In a blink, Zaos was on the elf, the scrawny neck in his hand, ready to slice his throat. Even at his death, Tel refused to back down.

"Who are you?" Tel ground out through his clenched teeth.

Zaos gave him the truth. "I am the son of a dark elf couple who mated for love and carry no hate in their hearts."

Tel spit to the side. "Weak then. You shame us, you and your unworthy family."

Fury erupted inside Zaos's chest and he raised his sword to put an end to evilness that would bring no good to anyone.

"Halt, do not kill him." Zaos froze on hearing

the king's command. "We need his weapon in our fight against the dragons."

Disgust in his mouth, Zaos threw his sword down. When Tel smiled, Zaos wanted to squeeze the jerk's throat, but he loosened his grip.

"I said let him live." Wrath wrapped the ruler's words as his hands lifted and shot magic at him. Zaos didn't understand. He had relented. When the magic flew over his head, he turned to see where it went.

Right behind him stood one of Tel's men with a dagger in a raised hand, about to stab into his back. He'd snuck up on them, coming out of the forest.

The king's magic struck the elf, shoving him through the air to drop him onto the dirt of the dead land. The elf screamed as he jumped to his feet. With his first step, his back foot disintegrated, the leg bone piercing the soft ground. His resounding shriek rang through the valley.

The elf fell onto his hands and knees. In a heartbeat, his hands melted away, leaving stubs at the wrists sinking into the dirt. He fell onto his side, his body flailing on the toxic surface. From there, he slowly dissolved into the dirt the same as rain from the sky sank into the thirsty grass.

The screams stopped when half of the doomed elf's body liquefied. The other side fell limp, disappearing into the ground as the first part had.

Growing up, Zaos, like all the others, heard the stories about the dead land and how it would poison anything touching it. Even the air. But nothing had prepared him to see the grisly death of how the land claimed flesh. It made him ill.

The king's voice thundered toward him. "You dare to act against my command, Tel?"

Zaos whipped around to see Tel had regained the splintered part of his sword, but he hadn't moved to strike. Tel's fingers released the destroyed metal. The defeated elf scooted away, climbed to his feet, then ran into the woods.

He would return after he sulked, only his pride wounded. But there would be retribution in the evil elf's heart set on destroying Zaos. He needed to watch his back more than ever.

The crowd dispersed and returned to their duties. On his way back to the caves, Zaos saw a few of the boys laughing hysterically. His path carried him close enough to speak. "What is so funny that you howl like banshees?" he asked.

The boys' laughter cut off upon seeing him.

They stood motionless, staring wide-eyed at him. Dwarf shit, if that didn't scream *guilty*, nothing did. "What have you boys done?"

They all turned to the tallest in the group. Zaos had seen the child around. He was at the age where it was time to leave the realm of carefree and enter the world of adulthood. The boy certainly should know right from wrong, but by the looks of the younger shamed faces, he had not chosen well.

The shine of defiance danced in his eyes. Same as Tel. Zaos sighed. No matter how hard he tried to be like his kind parents, too much of the darkness that always waited for his mind to weaken overshadowed him. Most elves, like Tel, allowed the emptiness to consume them. He wouldn't give in. Not yet anyway. The boy was well on his way into the blackness that ate the heart as surely as the dead land devoured its latest victim.

Zaos held his ground, forcing back the dark that made him want to strike down the insolent child. "Answer me." His eyes drilled the youth's, the spark of rebellion gone.

"Nothing," he replied. "We were just running around through the woods."

One of the others added, "Really far from here."

When no one else spoke, Zaos bellowed out, "*And*." The younglings started to cower.

The littlest of the group shouted, "Ryo followed us and we hid then ran back."

Zaos searched the area for the younger Ryo. "Where is he?"

"He's still there as far as we know."

Ryo was barely old enough to find his way from the clearing to the cave, much else "really far from here" as the one boy had said. Now the child was lost and on his own.

"Come with me, now," he ordered. The boys scurried toward him. They'd assemble a search party to retrieve the child before one of the light elves found him. May the Powers watch over the youngling.

CHAPTER EIGHT

After the break fast meal, Chelsea sat back in her chair, stuffed. The food was exceptional, yet it had no spices or butter lathered on. How could something in its raw form taste so good?

Wren leaned toward her. "You gonna eat those carrot things?" she asked.

On Chelsea's plate, a few orange, vegetable-like stalks remained. She pushed her dish toward her cousin. "You can have them. I ate too much." She hadn't felt this miserable since last Thanksgiving when she overate on sweet potato casserole and mashed potatoes.

"Velatha," Chelsea said, "how long do you think until Avery gets back?"

The elf woman had sat quietly and listened to the cousins banter through the meal. Chelsea was sure the woman didn't understand half the stuff said. Hell, most of the time, *she* didn't understand what they were talking about.

"I do not know. It could be any time soon or far away."

Yeah, not much help there. "I'd like to go for a quick run to help digest some of this food. Is there a trail I can follow that won't get me lost?"

"Yes," Velatha replied. "Go to the creek and turn toward the morning sun. Shortly, you will come to a path that leads to the mountains." Vel frowned. "How far do you plan to run?"

"Not that far, a few miles," she replied.

The elf's smile returned. "Yes, take that path then. Do not go too far or you will approach the land of the dark elves and dragons."

That didn't sound good. "How far is their land?" Chelsea asked.

"It is a sun-cycle ride on horse from here."

Assuming a sun cycle was a day, Chelsea wasn't worried. On a horse, a whole day riding could equate to thirty miles, at least. A full marathon was only twenty-six miles. There was no way she could run that far. She stood and headed in the direction Velatha pointed.

"I'm going for a run, guys," she said, looking back at her cousins. "I'll be back in little bit. If my sister returns before I do, y'all just hang out." Chelsea made her way to the creek, stretching her legs and arms in the process. She ran this morning, and going by her body clock, that was almost ten hours ago. It was time anyway.

With a deep breath, Chelsea felt her inner strength come alive. Her bummed mood from not seeing her sister elevated, her legs energized, everything in her tingled. Wow, she'd never felt this good before a run. Foreplay maybe. That was the closest thing she could think of.

Coming to the creek, she jogged the edge following the direction Velatha said and shortly came to a well-defined path. She wouldn't have any problem staying on the trail. This was marked better than the ones in the state park she ran in.

Needing to burn the large amount of excess energy built up inside her, Chelsea rocketed off in a sprint. After her legs and lungs tired a bit, she'd fall into her regular marathon stride.

Maybe it was her endorphin-soaked brain, but

the trees seemed to whiz by. She did most of her running in a park with a crushed rock track. So perhaps she wasn't used to having objects so near to her when training. That could explain her reason for feeling like she was almost flying along.

Then again, it could've been the pollution-free air, being so immersed in nature, and no thoughts of her ex dragging her down.

It had been several months since her ultimate humiliation in the restaurant. Was she ready to hit the dating scene again? That would be a big *hell no*. She was so tired of the same routine over and over.

Getting dressed up with hair and makeup and heeled shoes. Then the same places with the loud music that you had to yell to hear over, cheap liquor that gave her a headache before she even got home, and the weird men who gave her looks that resembled those of Manson. How she met her ex was a miracle. From hell.

She shook her head, wanting to get rid of him. The best thing he did for her was to show her what she did wrong in a new relationship. The main thing being that if something seemed suspicious, that was because something was wrong and not to ignore her gut about those things. If the guy wasn't trying to impress her and be with her, then he wasn't into her like he should be. Something else was taking up his mind and time. Move on.

Her body finally tired enough for her to relax into her marathon stride. Her mind cleared of thoughts and her body hummed like a plane engine cruising at five hundred miles an hour at thirty thousand feet.

The ground felt springy under her feet. Maybe the gravity was a bit lighter here than on Earth. Maybe magic made the ground feel squishy. The barely-there slippers her sister and the elves wore couldn't possibly protect their feet from anything.

Then she thought about what her grandmom had said right before she stepped into this dimension. The rhythm of her steady heartbeat went all screwy for a second. She had magic. But what did that really mean? Avery made the vine from a tree move, but that was it. It wasn't honorable to make food, according to her sister, not that she thought about making food with magic.

Magic wasn't making things float through the

air, was it? Wasn't that called telekinesis? What about bringing the dead back to life? No, that was called zombies and was totally gross if decaying body parts came back. That had to be shear made-up shit from a completely demented mind.

Thinking about all the Harry Potter books and what the girl did with spells, she realized that controlling the things around her to move seemed to be what the characters did most. Which was what Avery did, took control of something in the environment.

A noise caught her attention. She slowed and came to stop. She'd been running for a while, but wasn't winded or near being tired. That was almost like magic, too. Could magic affect her body—there the noise was again. It sounded like a child crying.

She stepped off the path toward the sobbing. Could there possibly be a lost kid this far from the village? If that was the case, then she would've thought the whole place would've been up in arms searching for the young one. Were there elves that didn't live in the village?

She kept her steps lights, trying not to step on a stick. Then she saw a plant with long tendrils that drooped over. The range of colors from yellow to red made her think of the flower that Ryllea described. It had to be a fire lily. She crouched beside it and studied it for a moment. Hard to believe something so small and simple could heal almost anything.

Hearing sniffling, she quietly made her way closer to the sound. Then through the trees, she saw the culprit. A boy—couldn't be any older than five or six, with snow white hair braided down his back. He sat against a tree with his head on his bent knees.

Chelsea stepped out from behind a tree. "Hey," she said.

The boy snapped his head up, sucking in a loud breath. His eyes were huge and filled with fear. She put her hands out to not scare him. "It's okay. I'm not going to hurt you. Hopefully I can help you. Do you speak English?"

She hadn't even thought about other species being on this planet. The boy looked humanoid. Except for his unnaturally white hair. It almost shined a silver.

"What's English?"

She then realized how stupid her question

was. She had to remember she wasn't on Earth anymore. "Never mind. You do understand what I'm saying." The boy nodded. "Can I come sit by you?" She had eased her way closer, step by step. Once again he nodded and she continued her slow approach.

She watched his eyes to see how close she could get. When they started to get wide, she stopped and sat.

"My name is Chelsea. What is yours?"

"Ryo."

"Why are you crying, Ryo?"

"Because they ran away. I don't know where home is."

"That wasn't very nice of the others, was it?" she asked. He shook his head. Shit. Now what did she do. She had no idea where he lived. "Do you live in the village with the elves?"

The boy looked at her with his head tilted. "Village?" he asked. "I live in the caves with the elves."

"The caves?" Nobody had mentioned anything about a group of elves living in caves. Great. She blew out a breath. "Well..." She looked around herself to note a dense population of trees for as far as she could see. She wasn't that far from the village. They could go there to see if anybody knew where the caves were.

"How about we go to where I live and I'll introduce you to the elf king. I bet he'd know how to get you home."

The child's eyes widened with fear again. "You are a light?" He started to get up.

Light? What did he mean by that? "It's okay. I promise not to hurt you." She scooted away to show him she meant no harm. The boy stopped, but his body remained tense.

"Why are you afraid of the *light* elves?" That was a new term for her. Avery nor Grandmom ever used that term—wait. Ryllea had mentioned the dark elves in the fire lily story. Her eyes trained on the little one.

He looked just like every other child on Earth. So what made him "dark?" Hell, his hair was white. You'd think it would be the opposite.

His small face scrunched up and he looked around as if spying to see if anyone was listening. "The bad king hangs us by our nuts."

A laugh spit out of her mouth that she covered with her hand and a cough. "That sounds horrible," she said after a moment of swallowing her laughter. "Who told you that?"

His narrow shoulders shrugged and delicate fingers fiddled with the pine needles on the ground. He needed the truth.

"Let me tell you how he really is, because he would *never* do that to anyone," she said, the kid's head slanted up enough for her to see his eyes under his hair. "The king's name is Tylen, and he's one of the nicest elves I know. He, uh..." What did the king do? "He plays with the children and makes them laugh." She nodded as he stared at her. "Oh yes. And the queen is so beautiful."

"What queen?" he said.

"Well," Chelsea replied, "she is somewhat new. But she's really nice, too. Oh, she plays video games really, really..." She let that trail off remembering she was in Crystal Kingdom. The kid would have no idea what a video game was.

"All right, let's forget that." She sighed. "I promise the king won't hurt you. You're with me and he likes me. So you'll be safe. Yeah?"

The boy did not look convinced one small iota. Chelsea wiped her face with her palm. "Okay, well then." She stood, startling the boy. "It's okay. I'm going to run to the village and ask if someone can tell me where your caves are and I'll come back and take you home. Is that okay with you?"

His tiny lower lip began to tremble, his eyes filling with tears as scrunched into himself. He whispered, "I'm scared."

Dammit to hell. Her heart broke into pieces at his beautiful, sad face. Again, she sighed and sat. "Okay, but how can I get you home if I don't know where to take you?"

With a shrug, he went back to fiddling with the fallen leaves. After a moment, he said, "I will hide. But don't tell the light king about me."

Her brow arched. "That would work, I guess." If it was possible to not to raise suspicion with such a question.

She stood slowly and held her hand out to him. He climbed to his feet and hesitantly put his little hand in hers. Chelsea couldn't stop the smile that spread on her face. He was such an angel. She led him to the path and they walked hand in hand.

"So," Chelsea said, "how did you get out here again?"

"I followed the others. They never let me go

with them. When they saw me, they ran away. I don't know how to get back." He sniffled.

"It's okay now. You're with me and you'll be home in no time." She hoped anyway. "Tell me about where you live. Is it nice?" He nodded then words sprouted from his tiny being. Half of what he said she didn't understand, mostly foreign words.

His free hand danced in the air as he spoke. He was one of those people who used their arms and hands when they talked. He was so adorable. She wanted to scoop him up and squeeze him to her.

A dark movement among the trees caught her attention. Her intuition screamed at her to run. She grabbed up Ryo, plopped him on her hip, then launched into the fastest run that she could with forty-five pounds on one side of her body.

Her heart pumped hard enough to hurt. Quite the opposite from marathon training.

Alongside her, the shadow kept up, but never passed for her to get a look at. If she turned her head, she'd lose her focus and probably fall. Too dangerous considering her cargo. Besides, if they were friendly, they wouldn't have snuck up on them.

Several yards in front of her on the trail, stick-like things dove from the air and stuck vertical in the ground, forming an obstacle to make her stop. Whatever was chasing them was intelligent, somewhat.

As she got closer to the barrier, she realized what created the line—arrows, as in bow and arrows that kill you dead. That thought scared the shit out of her. Today wasn't a good day to die.

Ryo's mouth moved, but the pounding in her ears was too loud to hear. Then he pointed and patted her chest. What did that mean? He stared into the trees where the shadow trailed her and pointed again. When he tapped her breastbone with his tiny hand, he looked into her eyes with a smile on his face.

Chelsea slowed and then could hear what he was saying. She didn't understand what the one word he repeated was. Sounded like "Darfin." But when a tall wall of muscle and white hair flashed to stand in front of her, she skidded to a stop, prepared to run the opposite way.

Behind her, another human-looking man jogged toward her, large bow held in his hand. She glanced into the trees to the side and saw many others surrounding her. She hugged Ryo to her protectively as the men closed in. The boy wiggled in her arms. Seeing that all the men had the same snowy hair as Ryo eased her mind. These males were probably the child's people looking for him.

She came to a full stop and Ryo squirmed to be let down. She trusted he knew what he was doing so she set him on the ground and he ran to the man in front of her.

Ryo hugged his leg, and he put a hand on the boy's back. His face set into a scowl. "Why were you taking the child?"

"Because he was lost. I was going to take him home," she said.

He took a deep breath, looked her up and down, then his eyes narrowed. "His home is in the opposite direction. What are you? I smell the elf and something I don't know."

The words of her grandmom flashed in her mind— keep to yourselves who you are, humans were horrible. Just as she was about to say she was from the village, she remembered the child's fright of the "light" elves.

"Uh," she mumbled, "I'm not going to tell you." She waved a hand in the air, scrunching her brows. "You've got your kid, now go on home. He's probably hungry."

From a pouch on his belt, the man pulled out a baseball-sized object. Ryo snatched it up and bit into it. Ah, food. Good.

The man looked at her. "Where were you going?"

Her insides shook. She didn't know how he would react. As it turned out, she didn't have to worry about what she said. Ryo said it for her.

"We were going to the light elf king where she lives," the little one said with his mouth full. "I was going to hide when she talked to him. She doesn't know where the caves are."

Chelsea shifted her weight from one foot to the other. She really didn't like this situation. The elves still surrounded her.

"Look," she said, "the child was lost because of *your* people," she pointed at him. "Not because of me. I was trying to get him home, but I had to ask how to get there. Now he's safe, so go on home."

She walked forward, passing the big elf. "Bye Ryo. Nice to meet you." She kept walking since no one stopped her. Behind her, she heard whispering voices. Sounded as if they were arguing. That couldn't be good if they hadn't left.

"Female, halt."

Those words set her into a sprint, but before she got in a step, both her arms were held. Chelsea fought and kicked, landing a perfect blow on a set of balls. Howling erupted then pain speared her skull and her world went black.

CHAPTER NINE

Zaos kneeled before his king. "You summoned, My Highness."

"Yes, the missing boy has been located. A light elf held him and was taking him to their village, according to what I'm told. The captor is in our hold."

"What would you like me to do, milord?"

"Question the light elf. Find out what you can on the village. How many young there are. The king's wellbeing. Do they plan to attack? I want to know all that is to be known."

"And after the questioning, sire?" Zaos asked.

The king tapped his chin for a moment. "Dispose of him on the dead land and report back to me."

"Yes, Your Highness." Zaos would gladly question the prisoner. And if he didn't get the answers he wanted, he'd beat them out. Nobody took a youngling away from their family. Anger grew in his heart, quickly consuming all of him.

The dark elves may not be the most loving species, but the children were cared for and given attention. And he thought the few females in the clan did love their offspring even if they didn't have traditional familial units. When a species was on the brink of extinction, they did what was necessary to survive.

Zaos's steps became heavier as they reached farther into the caverns toward the prison hold. If he didn't calm himself, he might kill the elf before he got a word out. Little Ryo must've been terrified. The youngling he liked. He was young enough that the other males hadn't started him down the dark path.

There was hope for Ryo and he would make sure the child had every opportunity to grow into a responsible, *nice* elf.

He took a deep breath before stepping into the hold to center himself. He would be fair and open-minded with the light elf before killing the bastard.

When he quieted, he heard a voice whisper on the air. It came from inside the holding cage and sounded like Ryo. But that didn't make sense. He poked his head around the opening to see little Ryo sitting *inside* the pen. On the floor was a body with strange clothing and the head belonging to that body rested in the little's one lap.

His tiny fingers stroked along the side of a face mostly hidden by long dark hair. Zaos's chin dropped. Who was this? Surely, not the one who captured Ryo. The king said it was a male.

He heard the child sniffle and mumble. "I'm sorry. Please wake Chelsea. Darfin shouldn't have let them hurt you. He's a good elf. But I'll protect you now. I won't let anyone hurt you. I promise. Just wake, please."

Zaos stepped away from the prison entrance and leaned against the wall. Confusion filled his mind with a score of questions. But he knew where to go to get answers.

Exiting the underground, he climbed the hill through the trees toward the dragon's land higher on the mountainside. Darfin would be guarding the northern edge, watching for sneak attacks and general dragon activity.

Zaos studied the invisible barrier separating

dragon from elf. The forest came to an abrupt end which was the only telltale sign. The upper slope of the rocky incline looked unoccupied, like a normal mountain. But it wasn't. That was what the dragons wanted others to believe.

The dragons' magic kept them hidden from outsider eyes. He had no desire to ever see a dragon unless on the end of his sword.

Zaos whistled the chronosis bird call, warning Darfin he was there and not to shoot an arrow through him. The elf dropped from a tree nearby. Together, they retreated down the mountain to a location safe for them to talk without being overheard by the overgrown lizards.

"Darfin," Zaos started, "what happened when you found Ryo earlier?"

The guard's face turned red, anger storming in his eyes. "You mean why is a female elf being held captive?"

Yes, that was more along the lines of the question that needed to be answered. By his guard's reaction, he wasn't happy with the situation either.

"When we came upon the boy's scent, another mixed with it. One I've not smelled. We took extra precaution in case the boy was in danger of being harmed by our presence."

"When we saw them walking the trail to the west, they were holding hands and our little one was talking like always. No fear was in the child. I had the men stand down, no weapons. We approached her from the forest and frightened her, for she grabbed the boy and ran."

"Zaos, she ran faster than all the men and with the boy holding to her. I barely kept up. I called out to her, but she either didn't hear me or heed me. She stopped because Ryo saw me running in the trees. She was the wind. Amazing."

"Ryo wasn't afraid. Why were they traveling west and not toward the caves?" he asked.

"She didn't know the location. Ryo said they were going to the light king so she could ask."

"The light king?" Zaos wondered what the demon's hell one of the light ones was doing all the way out there. "Where were they exactly?"

"Where the fire lilies end."

His brow raised. "Nobody, elf or not, need be that far from safety. Either side." He shook his head. He'd have to sit with the boys and tell them of the dangers of being so far away from help. There was no reason for them to be out there.

Zaos asked, "Do you think she had captured the boy and was taking him under the ruse of friendship to integrate into the village?"

Darfin sighed. "Perhaps, but she appeared genuinely concerned for the boy. Like most females with the children. She released Ryo when he wanted to come to me."

That surprised him, setting fire to his blood again. "Then why was she harmed? She lies unconscious now in the hold."

The guard stepped back, body tense. "I wanted her to go on her way, but Wiret argued, saying the king would be pleased with a female acquisition. The men agreed. I had no say in the decision."

Zaos crossed his arms over his chest. "So, we are willing to kill for stealing one of ours, but it's fine for us to take one of theirs." The disgust in him had reached its limit. He wasn't sure how much more he could take. Perhaps it was time to rethink his path in life.

He turned and headed to the caves. The female was an innocent and needed to be set free. He'd make sure no further harm came to her.

At that moment, Tel's image popped into his

head and fear stole into his heart. If that elf got his paws on the woman, she would be in worse danger than when six arrows were aimed at her.

CHAPTER TEN

The side of her face hurt like hell. Had she slammed into a wall with her cheek? She felt a soft touch brush down the other side of her head then heard a sniffle. Ryo came to mind immediately. She opened her eyes to look into a small pair of gray ones puffy from crying. Of course, he was upside down and looking down at her. Where was she?

With a groan, she sat up, making the room spin. Her stomach rolled along with it. Dipping her head down, the vertigo went away as did the urge to throw up.

"Chelsea, you all right?" a tiny voice asked. Ryo sat on his feet next to her with a hand on her shoulder. Such an adult sound coming out of a cherubic face was so adorable. She placed a hand on his.

"I'm okay. Are you hurt?" she asked. He shook his head. She leaned back against the wall. "What happened? Where are we?"

"Darfin found me. But the guards took you too. I told them you are good, but they don't listen to me." His head bowed forward, chin to chest. "I am sorry."

"Hey, now." Chelsea dragged him into her lap. "You are not to blame for any of this. The guards made the decision and there was nothing you could do about it, okay?" He laid his head on her chest and let out a sigh.

"Why are we in a jail cell?" she asked, just realizing she was locked inside a caged room.

He shrugged. "The guards put you here. I stay to protect you..." he paused for a second, moving his mouth, "okay." The word came out "whoa kay."

She smiled. "It's O." Her lips pursing into a circle.

His plump lips scrunched into a ring. "O. O. O."

"That's it. Okay."

He repeated the word over and over. Finally, she'd had enough.

"Okay, Ryo. You got it. Let's not practice for a while, okay?"

"Okay." He smiled, showing his straight teeth. She squeezed him against her. If only she could keep him.

"I bet your parents are worried about you. Have you seen them since we've been back?"

"There are no parents," he said as if that was a normal thing.

Wait. She didn't understand the plural "we."

"Do you have brothers and sisters?"

"There are others who have the same birth female as mine. Fathers could be any of the males."

As his words registered in her head, she became flabbergasted. Oh freaking god...the implications of what he said didn't bode well for her. Now she understood why they took her. They needed females to have babies. Just call her a handmaid. Nope, that wasn't happening.

Chelsea lifted Ryo from her lap, stretched for the door and pulled on it. There wasn't a lock of any kind, yet the bars didn't move.

"It's magicked," Ryo said. "Only strong magic can break it."

Well, shit. "I have magic, but have no idea how to use it."

"Why not? All elves know magic."

At that moment, an elf who sent shivers down her back came into the room. Chelsea and Ryo immediately stood. She instinctively scooted the boy behind her as the man's eyes slithered down her body, pausing on her T-shirt-covered chest.

"They were right," he said. "A female is here." His tongue wiped over his lips. "And you shall do more than perfectly." His hands went to his belt, undoing the hook.

The boy wiggled out from behind her, then stepped forward and pushed *her* behind *him*. "Go away, Tel," the little one said, crossing his arms in front of him.

The adult elf stood on the other side of the cage, glancing down at the child, then lifted his hand and made a fist. Ryo made a choking sound, his fingers at his throat. He wasn't able to breath.

Chelsea snapped her head toward Tel. "Stop whatever you are doing."

He ignored her, squeezing his hand tighter.

Ryo went to the ground, his face as red as ketchup.

"Stop it!"

The bastard grinned, watching the boy squirm on the floor. If the dickhead wanted to play rough, then she could give as well as take. She stepped toward the bastard and swung her leg through the bars, nailing him in the balls. He bent forward, smashing his face against the cage. Behind her, Ryo dragged in a breath.

She slid to the floor, lifting him and making sure his chest moved up and down.

"Are you okay?" she asked. Tears poured from young frightened eyes. If she ever got her hands on Tel, she'd choke the shit out of him and see how he liked it. As she hugged the boy to her, the door to the cage opened, slamming against the bars.

Nope. There would be no more touching the kid on her watch. Panicked adrenaline rushed through her, giving her strength and courage she normally wouldn't have.

Chelsea launched to her feet, stepped toward the elf coming at her, surprising him, and punched the heel of her hand in a solid upper hook to his chin. Tel's head snapped back and he stumbled against the bars. Chelsea didn't stick around to see what happened next.

She lifted Ryo and ran out the cage. When they came to an intersection, the boy pointed and she sprinted until he gave her another direction.

"That goes out," he jabbed his finger toward a rough-cut aisle in the rock, "but you must go fast to get past the guard."

Fast, she could do. She took a deep breath and focused. She imagined herself flying through the tunnel into the sunlight so fast that she was a blur to anyone looking. A twinge in her chest startled her and her legs felt as if filling with power. Too late to think about it.

She thrust forward with her thick thighs. Her hair whipped back from her face as if she stuck her head out the window in a car speeding down the highway. Her next blink, they were in bright light and flying through the air after hitting something hard.

CHAPTER ELEVEN

Zaos hurried down the mountain after getting the truth about the missing boy's recovery from Darfin. A voice in his head said he needed to get to the woman. Now. He didn't understand the why behind it, but the feeling was so intense, he couldn't wait. He'd figure it out after he reached the female.

Coming down the incline, he was near to a small entrance in the rock that would drop him close to the hold. He slowed, sliding on the loose gravel. Next he knew, he was shoved backward and had fallen on his ass among a group of scraggly bushes. Dual screams filled the air.

No thought on his part, his magic reached out and captured the two he hadn't initially sensed.

How did they move so fast? Why hadn't he seen them? What the hell was going on? He shook his head and sat up in the flattened section of bush to see what his magic captured.

Ryo was easy to recognize since he was upside down in the air, facing him. But the other was turned away, stretched out as if trying to catch their fall. The long, dark hair clued him in that this was the female in the prison—scratch that —*was* in the prison.

How did she get out? The cage had strong magic keeping it closed. Only a few elves had the ability to open it. He was one.

He set the two down, each lying in a different direction. Had his magic not stopped them, they would've gone over the cliff edge a few feet from where they rested.

The female rolled onto her back, her chest heaving up and down with each breath. His eyes were drawn to her shapely breasts under her baggy shirt. A feeling in his chest stirred. With a fist, he thumped his sternum. Indigestion?

Hand still thumping his chest and mind spinning trying to figure out what happened, he was unprepared for Tel's explosive exit. Before he realized what Tel's intentions were, the elf zipped to the female's side and kicked her hard enough to send her off the cliff. Ryo screamed, reached out, and disappeared over the side after her.

Once again, his power left him. It felt incredibly strange for his magic to act on its own. How could that be? He needed to speak with his father.

To stunned to move and knowing his magic had the boy and woman, Zaos watched Tel stomp away from the cliff, along the trail down to the hill's base. What the hell was that about? Did Tel want to kill her for escaping? He'd have to speak with the guard to make sure he understood women were not to be hurt, or elflings.

HE SET the escapees on the rocky ground gently. Both would've gone over a small cliff if he hadn't been quick.

The female rolled onto her back, her chest heaving up and down with each breath. His eyes were drawn to her shapely breasts under her baggy shirt. A feeling in his chest stirred. With a fist, he thumped his sternum. Hearing a growl coming from inside the cave, he was unprepared for Tel's explosive exit.

At elf speed, the man zipped to the female's side and kicked her hard enough to send her off the cliff. Ryo screamed, reaching out, and disappeared over the side after her.

Once again, his power left him. It felt incredibly strange for his magic to act on its own. How could that be? He needed to speak with his father. If he was losing control of his secret, then it might be time for him to leave.

Tel stomped away from the cliff, along the trail down the side to the hill's base. Why the hell would he want the female dead?

WHEN THE ELF was out of sight, Zaos called his magic to him, and the female floated over the side, the boy on her hip.

She looked sickly, but he could imagine falling to your death would have that effect on an elf. He climbed to his feet as the two came to a rest in front of him. Both stared wide-eyed at him.

The female stunned him with her beauty. He breathed deeply, confused for a moment from the familiar scent she had. Then he realized she was his mate. The witch had been right. He jerked back and tripped over a rock, landing flat on his back. He heard a giggle.

The female whispered to the boy, "Is that

normal? For an adult to keep falling on the ground."

Ryo replied, "Look at his feet. They're so big I don't know how he walks." The little one giggled again. "But Zaos is good. I like him."

Zaos sat up, scowl on his face. "I am not clumsy. My feet are in proportion to everything else on me."

The female straightened a bit. "Everything?" Her face went from pasty to full-on blush. He couldn't help the twitch at the corner of his lips. He smelled her arousal. The little one on her hip sniffed.

"What's that smell?" he asked.

Zaos lifted a hand and the boy floated from the woman's arms. "Time for you to go play, Ryo. And this time, stay away from the older boys. Play with those your age."

"But I'm protecting her," the young one said. Why would a child want to keep this woman safe? Every protective instinct in him surged on. If these two were in danger, he'd make sure no one touched them.

Whoa, where had that come from?

"I'll watch over her for you. You go play," Zaos said.

"Yes, sir." When his feet touched the ground, he shot down the trail as fast as his short legs would go.

Alone now, he released the small amount of power holding the female in place. She gasped and collapsed.

"What's wrong?" He dove to her side as she curled up on the ground. Her arms surrounded her midsection.

"What did you just do?" she whispered between shallow gulps of air.

"I didn't do anything. Just took in my magic."

"Give it back then."

He did and her body relaxed. He didn't understand.

She lay on her side, slumped but breathing normally. "I think that dickhead broke my rib when he kicked me. Your magic must be keeping the pain away."

Fire ripped through his body, igniting a rage like never before. Tel hurt his mate. The elf would not live much longer. She laid a hand on his arm and the insane intensity eased to a simmer.

"Thank you for saving us, twice." She sat up slowly. He gently scooped her into his arms and stood. "Whoa," she said. "What are you doing?"

Her hand grasped a handful of his shirt as she looked down.

"Don't worry. You're safe. I've got you."

She studied his face as he carried her. Damnation, did he have dirt on his face? Dragon shit, his hair was probably a mess. Figured that the moment the impossible happened, he looked like ogre dung.

When they stepped inside the small tunnel, he turned to the guard who he was sure witnessed the entire episode. "Keep this to yourself. I don't want anyone knowing." He put a bit of his power behind that last part to make sure the elf understood his intentions. The guard snapped to attention, saying nothing. Zaos gave a curt nod and continued forward.

"Are you taking me back to the jail cell?" His mate started to wiggle in his arms.

"No, mate. You are safe with me."

She instantly stopped moving. "Mate?" she said. "Why did you call me that?"

He smiled. She was as surprised as he was with the revelation. She was exactly as the witch said she would be. If only he had believed the gypsy that he would find his mate, he might have paid more attention to what she had said.

He'd been alive for hundreds of years and yet hadn't found his other half. He fully believed she didn't exist or died, never for them to be together. But here she was. He wanted to jump up and down, screaming his joy to the sky. Others would think he'd lost it. Not that he cared. He was too *nice*, anyway.

"When we're alone, and I will tell you what I know," he replied to her question.

Twisting and turning down the maze of tunnels, he arrived at his room. He lowered the shield blocking the entrance, passed through, and lifted it behind him. Looking around his place with new eyes, he was ashamed. This was not good enough for his mate. She deserved more and soon would have it. He'd give her every luxury she wanted.

He laid her on the bed and sat beside her. Worry shined in her eyes. "Where are we?" She scooted away from him. He took her hand and lifted it to his nose. He took a deep breath, memorizing her scent, letting it imprint on his soul. Then his fingers held tightly to her arm and he slowly ran his hand up her arm, then took her other arm, doing the same.

"We are in my room. Are you hurt anywhere

else?" He noted the tiny bumps on her arms that made the hair stand as she shook her head. She was affected by him. He repositioned on the bed to her legs and felt for injuries. How he wished she'd allow him to magic away all the material covering her skin. He wanted to feel her flesh against his, to take in her taste. He needed to reposition again, but for a different reason.

He looked over his shoulder toward the entrance to his room then turned back to her. "I might be able to fix you, but it requires me putting my hands on..." Fuck, just thinking about where his hands needed to go to heal her made him even harder. "Uh, on...you." The Powers! Did he sound like an idiot or what? She must think him a pervert.

She looked at him and sucked her top lip between her teeth. "If you keep your magic on me, will the pain stay away?"

"Yes, but it won't heal any faster than normal."

"That's fine. For now," she said. He didn't think she was ready for anything intimate yet. "My name is Chelsea Golby." She held her hand out.

"I'm Zaos Firefoot," he replied, shaking her

hand. "I'm sorry about all this mess. I had no idea any of this would happen in getting the boy back. How did you find him?"

"I was taking a run after eating too much this morning."

"A run?" he said. "You weren't on horseback?"

"No, that defeats the purpose of running," she answered.

The edge of his lips crooked up. "I see. Do you normally run that far?"

"What do you mean? How far did I go? I wasn't gone all that long."

"If you came from the light elves' village, which I suspect you did, then you traveled almost half a day's journey."

"But that's impossible," she replied. "I'd only been gone half an hour, tops." Her hands came up and covered her face. She mumbled, "Shit, this is so fucked up." Her arms fell back to her sides. "I need to go."

His body jerked at her words. She couldn't go. She couldn't leave him. He got up, magicked a bag into his hands and started tossing things into it.

"What are you doing?" she asked.

"I'm going with you," he said, wondering if he should take all his clothes or make more later.

"What?" she said, sitting up on the bed, "No, you're not."

"Why not?" he said, looking at her.

She spluttered for words. "Because I'm going to the light elves' village, like you said."

"And why can't I go, too?" His brows rose.

"Uh," she was quiet for a moment, "I guess there's no reason why you can't. I just..." Her eyes narrowed. "I don't know you. I don't trust you."

His heart squeezed. He should've expected that. The witch told him. "I saved your life twice. Is that not enough?" He hated how he sounded so desperate.

"Yes, thank you for that, but that doesn't mean you won't—" She cut off and he glanced at her. Her face flushed a soft rose. "You know."

If he had his way, he sure as hell would've done "you know." But his mate would take time and effort. She had to feel loved, the witch said. How the hell did he make her feel loved? He had been a soldier most of his life. He didn't *love*.

Dragon shit. He needed to talk with his dad.

"Zaos," Darfin stood outside the entrance to

his room, "are you in there? The king wants to see you and the female now."

Oh, shit. This was not good. He let his voice penetrate the shield. "We will be there shortly."

Darfin nodded, turned, then stopped. "Zaos, he's not happy."

CHAPTER TWELVE

Chelsea followed Zaos down the cave hall, trying to keep herself from thinking about his hands sliding up her arms and legs. She'd not felt anything so good in forever. She wanted to push him back on the mattress and do the same to him, but with her tongue. She tried to suppress the shiver going through her.

As they walked, he had his hand in the small of her back, guiding her. She was amazed how much warmth that simple act created. Her ex seldom touched her when they were together. Didn't hold her hand, never rested his hand on her back or leg. She hadn't noticed how starved she was for simple human contact.

What worried her was that he purposely didn't answer her question about the word "mate." Her grandmother had used that term all the time to refer to her husband. Did he think she was going to marry him? Pft. The boy was delusional.

But when she said she was leaving, with no questions, he started packing up his stuff. Who did that? Didn't he have a life here? Friends, family, anyone?

They came to a set of huge doors fixed into the cave wall. One of the two guards opened a side and Zaos walked her through. The room was breathtaking in a not so good way. Gaudy would be the right term with all the shiny silver and gold-covered items, huge gemstones, and stuff everywhere. Was this what they considered riches?

Stopping in front of the king, Zaos lunged onto one knee, yanking her hand to get her to kneel. That was a hell to the N O. Head bowed, he said, "My king, you wish to see me?"

The king stared at her for a moment then his lips curved up on the sides. "I see the story I was told is incorrect. It is a female with spirit we have captured taking the boy."

Chelsea's brow raised. "Whoa there, King.

Let's get one thing straight. I did not kidnap the child. I was trying to get him home."

The royal elf's eyes widened slightly, then a belly-busting laugh erupted from him. She glanced down at Zaos still in his bow. His forehead lay on his knee, shaking from side to side. What? She told the truth.

"Zaos, to me," the king said between breaths of laughing. Her escort immediately went to stand next to the throne. The scowl on his face told her he wasn't happy. Well, neither was she, dammit. "I am King Gorwin of the Dark Elves."

"I'm Chelsea." She didn't want to give her last name in case they knew of Avery. That could be a good thing or a bad thing. She'd save that card for later if needed.

The king breathed deeply. "What are you?" he asked.

Shit. That question again. She wished Grandmom would've given her something to say instead of telling her what not to say.

Zaos answered. "She's from the light elf village."

"But what smell is the other? I've not come across it in all my years."

She glanced at Zaos and his head twitched to

the side. Did that mean she shouldn't say? How did he know what she would answer anyway? More proof the big boy was hiding something. They'd discuss that later.

"It's my perfume," she said for lack of anything else intelligible.

He smiled again, but said nothing. He rose from the golden chair and stepped down to her level. "You are quite young." He circled her. She remained straight-backed, eyes forward. He wasn't going to intimidate her. "Your magic is hardly developed."

She snorted. "Big deal." Zaos dropped his forehead into his hand. Again, *what?* Magic meant nothing on Earth. The king stopped directly in front of her, invading her private space. She hoped his breath didn't stink. Did they brush their teeth over here or did magic take care of that, too? She really was clueless about this place.

He asked, "Why did you take the child?"

She pursed her lips, aggravated. She'd already answered that. So she'd ask a question now. "Why do you put the fear of god into the children about the light elves?"

The king stared at her and Zaos wiped a hand down his face. Was she making him sweat? The king turned, his cloak swishing around, and returned to his seat.

"The answer involves many factors, curious one," the king replied.

"The main being?" She saw Zaos's eyes widen. He slashed his hand over his throat, gesturing for her to shut up. Ha, not when she was being accused of something she didn't do.

The king looked back at him and Zaos dropped his arm. The man turned back to her and sighed. "As you've noticed, our home isn't as favorable to easy living as the village."

"Easy?" she answered. "They work for what they have."

The ruler sprang off his dais, into her face. His lips twisted. "Yes, but they don't live in a demon's hellhole with nothing but dirt around them. They're not worried about their children dying from rocks smashing them in their beds at night. They are not concerned about their magic vanishing."

Chelsea stepped back, searching for something to say. "Sounds like you have some issues to work on."

The royal burst into a sardonic laugh.

"Issues?" He walked back to his throne. "Yes, we have issues, little girl."

"Maybe I can help?" she commented. Zaos's eyes popped wide and he shook his head, face scrunched into a scowl. She ignored him.

That's what she did for a living. Helped people who couldn't find solutions on their own. It normally dealt with divorcing couples, but the problems here seemed domestic, too.

The king's forehead pushed up his hairline. "You think you can help? I've been trying for a millennium and you think the measly decades of summers to your life offer a solution?"

"Well, yeah." She frowned at the king's laughter. "I've been through a lot for being twenty-something." Almost thirty-something. "I'm an outsider looking in with a different perspective than you. I see things you don't."

He went quiet, staring at her. "If you can truly help us, I'll give you your freedom to return to your people. Give me your word you won't leave."

"Great," she replied. "I promise I won't leave. But let's say I can't make anything work. What then?"

"I will have you—"

The door to the room whisked open and the

bastard that attacked her and Ryo in the prison stomped in. She backed toward the throne, desperate for Zaos's safety.

"Tel," the king roared. The bastard went down on a knee.

"Pardon my intrusion, My King. I've come to claim this woman for my mate."

"No," both she and Zaos shouted.

The ruler swiveled around in his chair and looked at Zaos for a long moment. Whatever he was thinking, she'd never go with this dickhead.

King Gorwin turned forward. "I agree. No," he said. Tel's hands fisted into balls and a growl came from him. The ruler lifted a hand. "Be wary, Tel." The elf stopped growling, but anger still racked him. "The female has agreed to help us in two ways," he said.

Two ways? She only agreed to one. What was the other?

"In the past, I've ordered Zaos to spread his seed to strengthen our clan, but he has yet to obey."

Oh shit, she held her breath. If this was what she thought...

"I am giving him three days to impregnate this female. If he fails, I will give her to you, Tel."

CHAPTER THIRTEEN

Fear and joy ripped through Zaos as he stood next to his king in the throne room. The order to mate his mate was what he wanted, but he was sure she wouldn't be happy. Her inner elf wasn't normal. She needed more time to realize what he was to her.

She yelled, "Are you fucking serious?!" As her face turned as red as Tel's, Zaos hurried forward and grabbed her hand, dragging her toward the door. "I can't believe this. Even after I agreed to help you?" she hollered as he pulled her over the threshold and closed the door. "You prick!" she shouted at the wooden panel.

She slapped at his hand holding hers. "Let go of me."

He yanked her forward, his heart and mind spinning. There was no way he'd let Tel touch his mate. He'd kill the elf before that happened. He needed time to think. Taking turn after turn, he came to the nursery and pulled his unwilling cargo into the room.

"Mother, meet my mate, Chelsea. I need to talk with Father." He hurried out, too much crowding into his mind. The most important was how to protect his mate from Tel. The bastard had better stay away from her if he enjoyed being alive.

Outside the cave, he climbed the trail through the trees to find his father not far from the dragon's land. His senses went on alert for the enemy hiding, readying for an attack. He hated when his father worked this high.

Glancing farther up, he saw the break in the trees marking the property line. The dirt was churned up on the other side. Anger raced through him. Why did the dragons constantly disturb the ground to the point of weakening it?

"Son," he heard his father say, a touch of fear in his voice, "what's wrong? Is your mother all right?" His dad climbed to his feet at the crack in the ground he was measuring.

Guilt overpowered his anger. Shame for not visiting his parents more. Limiting his time to only when bad things were happening. He was one of the few with parents who were alive. He credited that completely to the fact they were true mates and loved each other.

"Mom is fine," he replied quickly. "I need to talk to you."

"Me?"

Zaos cringed at his father's surprise. Yes, he needed to spend more time with them. "I would like your advice."

"Mine?"

Zaos sighed. "Dad, stop making me feel like dragon shit."

His father broke into a laugh and clapped him on the back. The older elf found it difficult to reach his shoulder, but had no problem dishing out a mountain high of crap.

"Good to see you, my boy." He gestured farther down the incline. "How about a chair for your elder."

Zaos rolled his eyes. His father was always saying how ancient he and Mom were. Yes, they were as old as dirt, but just as capable as any other. He conjured a comfortable chair for each of them then sat hard.

Damn, where did he even start? "How's the crack?" He pointed his chin where his father stood moments ago. "This morning I reinforced the cave ceiling with rock."

His dad sighed. "That's good. The crevice isn't getting smaller. This one is deep and I worry about the soil's integrity. The dragons have to stop tearing up the ground."

"Good." Zaos hardly heard his answer. "Dad, I found my mate."

His father startled in the chair then jumped up to give him a hug. Guards were supposed to be hard-ass males with little emotion. But he was already accused of being "nice," so what the hell? He hugged his father.

"Congratulations. She will make you extremely happy. After she drives you insane."

His brows popped up. "Is that normal? I've known her a fraction of a sun cycle and I'm lost as to what to do with her."

The old man laughed. "Yes, a perfect mate for you." Both men returned to their seats. "So," his father said, "you want to know how to make her like you."

Zaos's eye met his father's. "How did you know?"

"Let me ask this," his father said, "does she like you at all or would she rather string you up by your nuts?"

He thought back to the moment they ran into each other outside the cave entrance. She was grateful for his help and he smelled her arousal. In his room, she was cordial. It wasn't until they talked with the king that he saw the true side of his mate. And dragged her out of the room before she got both of them dumped on the dead land.

"I'm not sure if she likes me, but let's say there'll be a time when she doesn't."

His dad laughed again. "My boy, you'll learn 'a time' is most of the time."

Zaos ran his fingers through his thin hair. "How do I get her to like me quickly."

"Quickly?" Dad said.

Zaos didn't want to go into the three days he had to create a grandelf for him and Mom. Or the threat of Tel looming over him.

"She's a light elf and I don't want her to leave without me."

When his father didn't say anything, he looked at him. Dad said in a lower voice, "Is she as the witch said?" Zaos nodded, his eyes searching the area for additional pointed ears. Dad nodded, chin resting on steepled fingers.

"Your mother and I discussed this many summers ago. We wanted to be ready when the time arrived."

A bit of his anxiety eased knowing his parents had the answers he needed. He wanted a relationship like theirs. One where the two halves made a whole, neither half suppressed, but uplifted. Arguments were finished with sex afterward—not that he was telling his father he knew that about them. And the love for each other was unconditional and unbreakable.

His father sat back in his chair. "The most important thing to remember about your mate is to never take her for granted. Once she feels unneeded, unloved, she'll be gone. Show her how you love her. And saying it helps when you forget your marriage date."

Zaos couldn't help the laugh that burst from him. He remembered that day well. Dad forgot one summer and his lunch and dinner were burnt. Like scorched to the point you couldn't recognize what the food was.

"Always be near her and touching her somehow. Don't let her forget you're there and let others know she's claimed," his father advised. "Make time to spend with her, right now, at the start. Don't wait. Make the effort."

He could do that. He'd been granted three full days with her. His guards were well trained in their daily duties. They didn't need him to make sure they were alert to danger around them.

"Oh," his dad added, "tell her everything."

Zaos raised a brow. "Everything?" The older elf nodded. "What if it scares her away?"

The elder sighed. "If she loves you, she won't leave you permanently."

Fuck. That didn't build his courage. Move on to the next question.

"Dad, I don't know how—I don't even think she knows how—but my mate promised the king she'd help with the situation."

"Which situation is that?" Dad asked.

Hell, he didn't know. "I think in dealing with the dragons. I don't know how anything else could change. I mean, there is no land for us to go to. We're stuck in the caves. Our dwindling population, she is supposedly helping with by just being a female. She wasn't too happy when the king mentioned getting pregnant."

"Does she not want a family and children?" A slight look of horror flickered in his father's eyes.

"Be still, Dad. I'm sure she does. We just haven't talked about it."

"When are you going to talk about it? It should already be talked about!" Dad stood from his chair and paced.

"Dad, I had no idea you were so anxious to be a grandfather."

"Don't be funny," the older elf said. "This is a serious matter," he mumbled. "I need to speak with your mother." He waved his hand in the air as if to brush away all that talk. "What about this helping with the dragons? Help how?"

"That's what I'm asking you. What should the king do that he's not to stop this war between the dragons and us?"

His dad sighed and stared out toward the border. So many trees had been destroyed over the summers from them burrowing into the land, and of course, the damn storms. His eyes flickered to the south to make sure the sky wasn't darkening. Puffy white clouds floated in the distance. He breathed easy.

"King Gorwin, a long time ago, should have spoken with the dragon king to discuss how to make things better for both of us," his father said, a hand rubbing his chin.

"You are not joking. The kings have never talked? How can that be?" He couldn't believe this. The simplest way to a solution was never carried out?

"Be still, Zaos. Sit," Dad instructed. "Of course, they have talked. But it was a long time ago and I believe they fought before they reached the crux of the issue."

"Wonderful," Zaos groaned.

His dad raised a brow at him. "Is that another saying of theirs? You don't mean that, do you?"

"It's sarcasm, which means the opposite of what the word usually means," he explained.

"I don't understand half the stuff you say anymore anyway."

Zaos shook his head. "Dad, back to the dragons. Don't worry about me. I understand myself just fine."

His dad snorted then thought for a moment. "I think the king needs to make contact with the dragons to discuss the burrowing and expansion. Perhaps something can be done that we're not thinking of." His father sighed. "I don't know, but there needs to be a connection between species.

Something that links us with understanding of both sides." He glanced sideways at Zaos.

His eyes narrowed and a sharp pain stung in his chest whenever he thought about what he could accomplish if he wasn't so bitter. "No," Zaos growled. "I will never give them the satisfaction." He stood from his chair again. "I will die before I grovel—"

"What about your mate, Zaos? Will she have to die before you do what you are born to do? What if you wait too long?" His dad shook his head. "Where is she now?"

"I left her with Mom."

His father jumped to his feet, hands on his head. "You did what?"

CHAPTER FOURTEEN

Chelsea watched as Zaos rushed out of the room. How rude. Men. She turned to the woman holding an infant in her arms. His mother, obviously.

"Hi, I'm Chelsea." She put her hand out to shake and when the woman looked at it, Chelsea snapped it back. "Sorry, habit." Talk about awkward. She couldn't think of anything not stupid to say.

The woman lay the baby in a crib, no expression on her face, then came back and took Chelsea's hands in hers. "I've prayed to the Powers for many summers to bring you here."

Well, shit. What did you say to that? "Umm, thank you?"

His mom dropped her hands and enclosed her in a hug. "My name is Hycis," she pulled back, leaving her hand on Chelsea's shoulders, "but please call me Mom."

Chelsea closed her eyes and took a deep breath. She said, "He called me his mate." Her eyes opened and she fought the tears she was unprepared for. She understood from Grandmom that a mate was the one created to share your life with. A soul mate. The perfect person, or elf, for her. Avery and Tylen were mates. Did she have that right? "What does that mean here?"

Hycis led her to a pair of chairs at the front of the room. When she was situated, his mother started. "A mate is the one person who will make you want to pull your hair out, and will still love you when you're bald."

That was not what she was expecting. A laugh burst out and she slapped a hand over her mouth to not wake the sleeping babies.

His mother smiled. "I am being humorous," she said. "But that is near the truth. Especially with Zaos."

Oh shit. What did that mean? "Why is that?"

"Zaos is a natural born leader. But he refuses to take on that roll any more than the king has made him. He is second to the king only, which means he's used to being obeyed even if he is wrong. There will be times when you'll want to throw him on the dead land for being dwarf-headed."

Chelsea assumed *dwarf-head* equated to pig-headed.

Hycis's face turned serious. "When did you and my son meet?"

"A couple hours ago."

"I am sorry. I do not know what an *hour* is." Hycis clasped her hands together, laying them in her lap.

"Right," she mumbled, "I forgot. Soon after the break fast meal."

The elf's face sagged with a frown. A sharp zap of fear struck her. The woman shook her head and the smile returned. Should she ask what that was about?

Mom said, "You have not been together long enough to mate, then. Am I right?"

Chelsea felt her face set aflame. The woman was asking if she'd had sex with her son. Oh god. Could this get any worse? "We haven't been alone." Hopefully that would suffice as an answer.

The elf leaned toward her and patted her

hand. "You need to know that as your mate, my son will love only you until the day he no longer breathes. Other women will never enter into his mind. When he is with you, you will be the center of his world. The only thing he wants is to make you happy, even though he'll fail many times."

"Why will he fail?" Chelsea asked. Was something wrong with him?

Mom smiled. "He is a male."

Chelsea smiled back. "'Nuff said." Both giggled. "I would like to ask you a question about something said about your son."

"Yes, please, ask me everything. It is important you understand all you can."

Well, that was a loaded answer. She'd start simple. "The king said Zaos had not spread his seed to strengthen the clan. What did he mean by that, exactly?"

"See, my son was loyal to you before you even met. Trust him."

That answer didn't help much.

Hycis stood and whispered, "Come with me."

The two walked closer to where the babies slept. Chelsea counted three cribs which held infants of different ages between newborn to toddler.

"These are our future along with the other groups of young ones. Ten in total."

Chelsea wasn't sure she understood what the woman was getting at. "So, you have ten children in the whole community? That's it? How many live here?" The light elf village had a ton of people gather for breakfast. A couple hundred maybe. They all had been away doing their jobs when Chelsea and her cousins arrived, so the place looked almost abandoned. Like this place had looked all morning, too.

"We have thirty-five full grown males, four who think they are grown males, and the ten young ones, including these."

Chelsea's jaw dropped. "Forty-nine? You have forty-nine total people in this clan?"

"There are four females, including me. You will make five."

Yeah, hold the phone there, missy. She wasn't sure about all this baby making. "I haven't decided—"

Mom frowned. "But you are my son's—"

"His mate. Yeah, I know that. Why are there so few of you? Can't the mates—" then she realized what it meant to only have four, or five, women. There were no mates. Ryo had said he didn't have parents, but the implications didn't

123

occur until this second. The community raised the children.

When she said she didn't want to be a baby machine, she meant with Zaos as the father of all her children. But that's not how it worked here. Now she understood why the king said she would go to Tel if Zaos didn't impregnate her in three days. The fathers literally could be anyone. Holy shit. That was so *not* happening with her.

Hycis put a hand on her shoulder. "You look ill. Come sit." Mom helped her back to the chair. "Are you all right?"

Chelsea waved it away. "Yeah, I just put some things together in my head."

"You have no worries. You are a true mate. No one will touch you."

Not according to the king. She blew out a breath. "Why don't the men go out and find someone they can marry?"

The older woman scowled. "King Gorwin will not allow others into the clan. No fae, no goblins, no light elves."

"I'm a light elf," she said. "Why hasn't he kicked me out?"

"You are beautiful, daughter. Plus, my son is interested in you. He has not shown feelings for any other woman, nor has he shared his bed for that purpose. The king wants Zaos's offspring badly. He is the biggest and strongest of all elves. That means you stay, light or not."

Yup, Chelsea didn't miss the "daughter" reference. It was kind of nice seeing that she and her stepmother never had a favorable relationship. She liked this woman.

"But..." his mother said and stopped. Her dark eyes glanced toward the entrance of the cave room.

"But what?" Chelsea replied.

"Make my son tell you of his first days of life," Mom answered.

Chelsea was about to ask more when Zaos and another elf entered the room. The man wearing a huge smile zeroed in on her. His arms opened and embraced her.

After a second, he said, "I really hope you are my son's mate or I've really embarrassed myself."

"Dad," Zaos whined. Chelsea giggled. The older elf was adorable. He fit perfectly with Hycis.

"I guess that means you are my new daughter," the elder said. "I am Klaern, the big whiner's father." Zaos rolled his eyes and leaned against the wall. Oh, she loved his family already. Odd that

Zaos was so much taller and bigger than both parents.

Zaos said, "So what has Mom told you that she shouldn't have?"

His mother frowned and slapped at him playfully. "Stop that. She's your mate and needs to know *everything*."

"I know," he mumbled. "Dad said the same thing."

Well, now. That was interesting. Seemed her mate had some secrets to spill and she couldn't wait to hear them. When she moved closer to him, he pulled her in and wrapped an arm around her. Exactly like his father did his mother. Chelsea snuggled into him. He felt so right, so safe and warm.

She wanted to run her hands over his chest, feel every ridge and valley of his muscled body. He dropped a kiss onto her forehead. Then she realized he hadn't even kissed her yet. She focused on his lips, wondering how they would taste. Her mouth dried with her desire growing inside.

After a deep breath, Zaos swung her toward the entrance. "Uh, we'll be outside for a while. I'm going to, uh, show my mate around."

As they walked out, she heard his parents

snickering to each other. Oh god. They assumed she and their son were going to have sex. A thrill burst in her stomach at the thought. His large, rough hands sliding along her skin...

She felt his body vibrate and he pulled her into a narrower aisle. He put her back against the wall and cupped the side of her face in his hand. His breath was hot on her throat. Hotter than she would've ever imagined. "Chelsea, the Powers help me, you smell so fucking good."

The kiss he whispered under her ear sent shivers through her. Oh god, her knees were about to give out. She pulled him against her. The vibration she felt earlier was from his chest. It almost felt like a purr. Felt good going through her, heating her lower stomach. Her hand lay aside his cheek, guiding him to her lips.

So soft, so commanding. The man tasted like sin. And she wanted to be very bad. This was her mate. The man born to love her and only her. Her heart wanted to jump in fully, trusting him with her life. But her brain threw on the brakes. The humiliation at the hands of her ex still stung. Didn't matter what *mate* meant. If the man didn't prove his love for her, she wasn't biting.

She pulled back from the kiss, licking her lips.

He sighed and rested his forehead against hers. "Chelsea." Her name sounded so sexy from his mouth. A slight tickle of awareness danced on her ribs. She realized how hard she was breathing and remembered that her mate's magic was keeping away the pain from were Douche Bag kicked her this morning. Shit. She'd forgotten about that.

She said, "You mentioned something about going outside."

His sex-on-a-stick smile nearly broke her defenses. He said, "I want to show you something."

Oh, and she'd gladly look at it, too.

CHAPTER FIFTEEN

Outside on the rocky incline, Zaos led his little mate by the hand to his favorite place. He wanted to be alone with her. Be close to her. Show her how much he cared for her already. She didn't know what being a mate meant.

Back in the nursery, the smell of his mate's arousal had sent him over the edge. He pulled her into a less-used hall and tried to keep himself from mauling her. He wanted nothing but to be lost in her. She affected him completely in the few hours they had known each other.

"Zaos," she said, "since I volunteered to help with solving the elves' problems, could you tell me what they are exactly? What's up with fighting the dragons?"

He gripped her hand tighter. At least this question didn't require him to reveal something he'd kept secret for hundreds of years.

He started, "A long time ago, in a dimension far, far away..." He glanced back at her narrowed eyes and gaping mouth. He laughed. "I'm joking. That's the wrong story."

"But—how—"

He lifted a hand to quiet her. "Let me tell it my way or I won't tell it at all."

She slid her fingers across her lips and acted to toss away the key. He laughed and swept her up and swung her around. "I guarantee you sealing your lips against me won't last." He pecked a kiss on her nose and set her down. "Come on. We have a long way to go."

He continued the trek across the side of the mountain. "Back to your question, my love. The dark elves have several issues, I'm sure you noticed. But the only one I can see that could possibly be changed is the relationship with the dragons. And I don't see how that can really change either. It's a vicious circle no one can stop."

"Start with why you're fighting the dragons in the first place."

He snorted. "That's easy. Land."

"Land?" she questioned, "As in who owns the most?"

"For the dragons, yes," he answered. "For us, it's more like what is needed just to survive here."

"I don't understand."

"When the dragons sleep or during a storm, they burrow into the ground like a snake. They churn up the dirt, destroying any flora and disturbing tree roots to the point they die. This whole mountain at one point was covered in forests. Now, where you see rock is where the dragons have lived."

"So you want to stop them from annihilating the trees and forests?"

"Yes and no." They came to a deep divide in the ground.

"Holy crap," Chelsea said, looking into the gap. "How far down does this go?"

Zaos felt the heavy sadness mixed with anger creeping into his chest. "It nearly splits the mountain. It's where we lost half our people."

"What?" his mate gripped his hand. He held her tightly to him, his nose buried in her hair. Her essence absorbed into him, calming his emotions that wanted to rip out of control to rage and seek revenge for those they lost. Instead, he lifted them over the chasm with his magic and set them on the other side.

Her little "eep" when her feet left the ground was so cute. He loved everything about her. Every single thing.

"Keep talking. You've got two stories to tell now," his mate said when he only wanted to retreat inside himself. She was good for him.

"Yes, my love." He kissed her forehead. "Actually, they are part of the same tale. The dragons are rather large in size, depending if they are male or female. But the females aren't something to sneeze at. So when they dig themselves in, they go deep, all the way to the bedrock underneath."

"You mean the rock of the mountain? All this we see?"

He nodded. "Yes. Their weight cracks the rock, weakening it to the point of collapse."

Chelsea gasped. "In the caves." She stopped, pulling his arm back. "That's how you lost your people? They died in a massive cave-in?"

The tears in her eyes touched him. She already cared for a people she knew nothing about. A people who'd shown her little else than anger and hostility.

He nodded. "That was long ago and our clan never fully recovered. The hatred for the dragons is strong."

"Obviously, no one has had tried to talk to them about finding a solution," she said, more to herself than him.

"You'd think, but I don't know. We keep moving along the caverns in the mountain to find stable places. The dragons move along the surface as the dirt is washed away in the storms. Without the trees and grass to lock in the ground, it erodes very quickly. We look for and monitor cracks. That's what my father does. He keeps an eye out for potential problems."

"So the reason for fighting is to keep the dragons from taking the ground over the caves."

"Yes, basically. But they continuously ease their way lower and lower. I don't understand why they think they have a right to the whole mountain." He shook his head. "All right, no more of that talk. We're here."

He guided her over a hump of rock to see a waterfall oasis in the middle of the barren rock.

"Oh." Her eyes got larger as she took in the

sight. That was his first reaction when he came across the place accidentally. "This is beautiful." She scrambled down the steep side toward the base of the fall.

The height wasn't as grandiose as others on the planet, but it was enough. The water came out of the top of the cliff wall, seemingly from nowhere. He'd tried to find the source, but never did. After a while, he gave up and accepted the peace it brought him.

The pool at the bottom was colorless. Almost like glass if not for the waves created by the incoming water. As they got closer, he felt the spray of the mist on his face. It cooled him on hot days, refreshing his tired body and mind.

Grass and a few trees covered the ground surrounding the stream that carried the current. Oddly enough, the water disappeared back into the mountain under a pile of boulders the water moved there fifty feet away.

Chelsea dragged him to a shady spot under a tree near the pool. He sat with his back against the trunk and sat her between his legs to lean against him. This was perfect. She snuggled into him and he wrapped his arms around her stomach, carefully hugging her to him, making sure he didn't hurt her ribs.

And demon's hell.

Now was not the time for his dick to decide to show up for the party. She'd probably think he was a sex fiend. But with her ass pushed against his crotch, there wasn't much he could do about it. All of him wanted all of her.

"Wow," she said. "Avery would love this. Too bad she's not—"

Her abrupt stop tilted his head toward her. "What's wrong?"

"My sister," Chelsea replied. "I've been gone for hours. The whole village will probably be looking for me soon, if not already."

He was confused. "Don't they know you came all the way over here?"

"How far away are we? I didn't run that long."

He remembered this morning when he was entering the small entrance and she burst from the opening. He hadn't seen her or even smelled her until his magic grabbed her by the cliff. Not even full elves could move that fast.

"Your magic," he said. "Were you using it when you were running?"

"My magic?" She remained quiet for a moment. "My grandmom mentioned that I had magic, but she didn't say anything else. I've never used it. Didn't know I had it."

"That can't be right," he said. "I feel it. It isn't buried. You've been using it for a while."

"But—" she turned to look up at him, "when? I can't make stuff float in the air or conjure a rabbit from a hat."

"That's not what magic is about," he told her. He leaned forward, kissing her scrunched brows. "Magic comes from the heart. The place where your love comes from." He poked her chest over her heart. "Naturally, whatever you love, you're going to put more of your heart into."

She kissed his jaw. "Your words are very poetic, dearest, but I have no idea what you're getting at. Make. It. Simple."

He turned her so her back was against him, pulling her in tightly. "I'm saying that you used your magic when you were running and traveled much farther than you intended."

"I ran the same as I always do at home," she said.

"And therein lies the difference. Here, you are surrounded by magic, you breathe it, touch it, eat it. It becomes a part of you. Here you can wield great power while not exhibiting a thing elsewhere."

"Oh my god. Are you saying my magic made me run faster and farther than normal?"

"Yes." He laid his head back against the tree. His mate was highly intelligent, but this magic stuff, she wasn't grasping.

"Will they come this far to look for me? I need to go back to tell them I'm okay." She started to stand and he held her down.

"I got a better idea," he said. "You have a sister at the village, yes? I thought I heard you mention one."

"I do. Avery." She tilted her head back to look at him. "Does her name sound familiar?"

He smelled a hint of worry from her. "No. Should it?" He scoured his brain, searching for any recollection of that name.

She relaxed against him. "No. Never mind. What has my sister got to do with anything?"

"Family naturally has a psychic connection. Add your magic to it and you two can talk all day without hanging up."

"Wow. Okay. Let's do it. What do I have to do?" She blew out a breath.

"Relax, for one thing." He rubbed her shoulders, feeling the tension and knots. Pressing his thumbs down, he gently worked the tight bundles loose. His mate groaned and his dick got hard so quickly, he felt lightheaded. The damn thing thumped with his pulse.

He gritted his teeth to resist any temptation to touch her more than he was. He would die soon if he had to keep this up. "Breathe in," he said. Her shoulders lifted as her lungs filled. "Hold it. Hold it. Hold it. Now let it out slowly through your mouth." She deflated.

His fingers made their way down her arms and over her shoulder blades. He tilted her head backward to rest in his hand. From there, he massaged her temples, running a thumb over her forehead. "Another breath in. Hold it. Let it out." He laid her head against his chest.

"How do you feel?" he whispered.

"Like I'm a bowl of Jell-O."

He chuckled. "Good. Now we're going to find your magic."

"Find it?" she asked.

"Yes." He crossed his arm in front of her to tap the area above her left breast. "Feel the beat," he breathed. *Tap tap. Tap tap. Tap tap.* He noticed his pulse timing with hers.

"Think of your sister. Picture her in your mind." His fingers kept tempo. *Tap tap.* "Call out to her with your mind. Let what you're feeling flow out of you." *Tap tap.*

He closed his eyes and opened his heart to let his magic do as it would. He wanted to join his mate in what she was seeing, but he didn't know if that was possible. When the image popped into his mind of a woman who looked a lot like Chelsea, but wasn't, he'd hoped they had connected.

Now all he had to do was get her to come out of her mind before her magic decided it liked this untamed freedom.

CHAPTER SIXTEEN

C helsea relaxed into Zaos, letting his fingers soothe her into a hypnotic state with only the beat of her pulse in her consciousness. *Tap tap. Tap tap.*

Her chest tingled where Zaos's fingers touched. The tingling spread through her until she was nothing but abuzz with energy. Finding herself in darkness, she felt a presence next to her, but didn't "see" anyone. She didn't need to to know who it was.

Zaos's heart was open with his magic and she could feel the love he had for her. It startled her, being so strong so quickly. Comfort and security surrounded her, giving her confidence and taking away the fear usually accompanying first times.

The image of Avery came into her head. Her sister was frantic, pacing with their cousins and Tylen and his men discussing something serious.

"Avery," she called out. Her sister stopped and looked up. "Avery, it's me, Chelsea. Can you hear me?"

Her sister fell to her knees, fingertips on her temples. Tylen was at her side in a blink. They talked, but she couldn't hear them.

"You are not connected completely?" Zaos voiced to her. "Her mate will help her understand how to find her own magic and you. Patience."

She thought to herself, "Yeah, great. The one thing I suck at—waiting."

He chuckled.

She ducked her head. "Oops, guess my private thoughts aren't that private at the moment."

More warmth, comfort, and safety closed around her, filling her. Zaos kissed her hair. "I am sorry, my love. I don't intend to interfere. I believe this is how we will talk to each other when we're apart after we are mated."

"You mean we can telepathy with each other?"

"Yes, that is...a way to say it," he answered. She could feel his laugh at her word choice. Jerk.

"Your jerk," he whispered.

"Damn straight. Don't forget it." Her heart felt happy, light—

"CHELSEA!" bellowed through her head. She slapped her hands over her ears. As if that would really help.

"Chill out, sis. I'm okay."

"WHERE ARE YOU?"

"Avery, tone it down. Is Tylen with you? In your head?"

"Yes. I am here. Good to know you have found your magic, sister," the elf king said.

She squeezed her mate's hand. "I had a lot of help. Sis, Tylen, this is my mate, Zaos."

"WHAT?" thundered in their magical place. "Sorry," her sister said, "I accidentally yelled that." Avery stared at Zaos. "Really? Your mate?"

Tylen leaned toward her. "It makes sense, my love. Your and your sister's blood magic would call the same beings as mates." Narrowing his eyes, Tylen turned to Zaos. "You are a dark elf, is that true?"

"Yes," Zaos replied. Chelsea felt him tense beside her.

Tylen frowned. "You are something else, also."

"Yes." With his reply, Chelsea felt nervousness and fear from him. This "something else" must've been what his mother was talking about. She tried to send him calm emotions, letting him know whatever it was, it would be okay.

Tylen continued. "As the mate of Chelsea's sister, it is my duty to watch over her as family until she is mated. And after if I believe she is being treated—"

"No worries, Tylen, king of the light elves. As her mate, I will take special care to protect her before and *after* we mate. She is in good hands."

"Chelsea," Avery said, "when are you coming back? And where are you now?"

"I am with the dark elves in their home—"

A glow faded up around Tylen. Chelsea felt a strong vibration come from him. "Did they take you by force?"

Zaos stepped forward, tucking her behind him, his own glow vibrating. "She is here willingly. Now, anyway. It is a long story she will share with you later. Now we are here to inform you that she is safe and you do not need to worry."

Tylen gave a nod. "I know the reputation of the dark elves—"

Avery grabbed his arm and whispered, "Why don't I know it?"

Tylen turned his head slightly. "Worry not, love." He raised his voice. "What I see in this dark elf has not existed in over a thousand summers." Tylen bowed his head. "I trust his word. As of now."

"Avery, we'll be back in a couple days. There are some things I'm helping them with. I promised to stay until then."

Her sister still looked worried. "That's fine," Avery replied. "But that doesn't mean I can't come to where you are."

Tylen snapped his head around to her sister. "This we will discuss."

Zaos's essence wrapped around her. "Love, it's time to go."

"How do I get out of here?"

"Think about the waterfall and being with me there. Tell your magic that's where you want to be now."

"Gladly. Bye, Avery. Love you."

She opened her eyes to the tranquil sight of water cascading over a cliff. She spun around on his lap, overexcitement racing through her. "Oh my god! We did it. We really did telepathy."

"It's mag—" he started, but she threw her arms around his neck and kissed him. She wasn't thinking anything sexy about this kiss. But her mind changed quickly. He tasted so damn good, and felt incredible pressed against her. She could do this forever. His strong arms squeezing her, his powerful legs thrusting his hips in and out of her.

Damn, that sent a flame of heat to her lower stomach. Her mate growled. He must've known when she was hot for him. His reaction was too dead on.

He grabbed her waist, lifted her, then set her down to where she straddled his lap. Shit, fuck, damn. His hard-on lined up with her clit. Her hips, on their own volition, rubbed against him. His breath hitched. "Chelsea" whispered through the air. He was her mate, the one for her, and sex was all right even though they didn't know each other that well. In theory.

When Zaos pulled her back, disappointment and a touch of relief rolled through her. This wasn't the time for that.

"Chelsea, this isn't the right time for us to mate. But believe me when I say I want nothing else right now." His heavy breathing confirmed to her that was the truth.

She sat on his legs. "You know, there isn't a guy out there who would've thought about my wellbeing over their cock." When his cheeks reddened a touch, she smiled and kissed the warm flesh.

"Is that a good thing or bad?" he asked.

She laughed. "It's good. Very good. Now, tell me about the first days of your life."

CHAPTER SEVENTEEN

Any sexual desire in him was sucked right down the drain with the force of a tornado. Sitting under a tree with his amazing mate straddling his lap, Zaos stared into her eyes, wondering if there was a way he could get out of telling her what she deserved to know.

The waterfall spray floated in the air, creating iridescent rainbows against the dark boulders. He could toss her into the water then let her drown him, but that wouldn't be enough to distract her.

He sighed, trying to keep the sadness from his eyes. His mother always told him she could read his every emotion through his eyes. He'd tried to change that, but he felt so strongly, so passionately, that he simply couldn't contain it all inside.

Chelsea straightened on his lap. "We don't—"

"No," he said, holding her in place. "We do need to do this. You are my mate, my only love. I trust you with my deepest secrets that could bring about my death. You deserve and need to know all this so you make the right choice in deciding if you'll stay with me."

Her quiet gasp drew his eyes to hers. Yes, she had a choice and he wanted her to know that. Just because they were mates didn't mean the human half of her would like him. That was the part he had to win over with honesty and devotion. He knew he wasn't worthy of her.

"Will you rest against me while I tell you everything?" he asked. When she nodded, he scooted her forward on his thighs until her body leaned on his, her head lay over his heart.

"It's not a long story, but it's hard for me, the badass dark elf guard that I am..." he got a smile out of her, "to admit to being vulnerable. Others find out stuff like this and they will eat you for breakfast. The tough killer façade has to become a part you even if it's not who you are."

Fuck, he was stalling with this dragon shit. *Just spit it out, boy.*

"My parents that you met are not my birth

mother and father." He felt her body jerk slightly. "My father—Klaern—told me he was on the mountain working when a woman with long black hair appeared from a mist and handed him a baby boy. She told him the mother was dead and the birth father didn't want him." His voice cracked on the last four words.

Pain that he'd kept bottled up for centuries spread in his chest. He squeezed Chelsea to him to prove she was there. That she hadn't left him yet. He lowered his head to bury his face in her hair. Fuck, he hated this. Why, after so damn long, did this still hurt so much?

He waited until he could speak strongly again. "Klaern's wife had just suffered a miscarriage, so he saw no reason to not take the child if there was no better choice. The woman said to cover the boy's duality with elf magic and his life would be blessed. She walked into another mist and disappeared."

Chelsea whispered against his chest, "What's duality?"

"Yeah, I'm getting to that." He dreaded to continue. What if she ran screaming from him? What if she told him she never wanted to see him again? Panic rose in him, choking his words. Was that him or his duality causing that?

"The three of us were a family just like all the others at that time. Though Dad told me later that they watched me carefully growing up for signs of something strange. They told me often to tell them if I felt something weird happening. But they could never tell me what was *weird*. At that age, I didn't know what normal was.

"When the time came for me to grow from a child to an adult, we discovered what that *strange* was." Surprisingly, he chuckled, looking back at the incident. "At this time, we still lived in the trees and had our full magic. We were seated for the evening meal in our home because Father had arrived from work too late to join the others.

"I was at the point where it was almost time for me to make a decision what I was going to do with my adult self. If I was going to be a guard, crop gatherer, or whatever.

"Sitting at the table, I started feeling something strange in my chest. As it grew, I felt as if I'd swallowed an ember from the fire. It took my breath. My body was enlarging as if I were a balloon. Then my bones started cracking, breaking." Chelsea gasped and her arms tightened around him. Hopefully, they would remain there.

"Of course, we were all freaking out, having no idea what was going on. Then suddenly I burst into this huge creature. The chair I sat in smashed to the floor under the weight and then I fell through the floor and landed on my big, huge ass on the ground."

Chelsea pulled away, eyes huge with questions and fear. "Oh my god. What happened?"

He laughed out loud, warmed by her genuine care. He pulled her back to him, she felt too good. "So, I looked up from where I sat on the ground and saw my mom's and dad's faces looking over the edge of the hole in the floor. Then as nonchalantly as anything, Dad said, 'Oh, he's a dragon.'"

He paused, waiting for her reaction. Would she run and this be the last time he ever saw her? His heart would crush with her loss. He wouldn't go on without her. His arms involuntarily tightened around her, but he didn't want to force her to stay.

She slowly pushed back until she sat facing him. Her expression held no fear, then her brows drew down and eyes narrowed. "Are you telling me you're an elf who can shift into a dragon?"

Shift wasn't the word he was thinking, but it would work. "Yes. My mother was an elf and my father a dragon."

Her eyes grew huge and her face blushed a lovely rose. He smelled embarrassment and disbelief. He needed her to talk. He asked, "What? Why are you flushed?"

Her face dropped into her hands. "I-I was just thinking, well, not really, but sorta, how do an elf and a dragon...you know... Aren't dragons really big?"

When it dawned on him what she was talking about, he threw his head back and laughed. She leaned forward and buried her face in his shirt. She mumbled, "I'm so mortified I even said that."

He lifted her shoulders and kissed her. Cupping his hands around her face, he smiled at her. Of all the things that could have gone through her brain, she focuses on how an elf and dragon mate.

He said, "I guess I should tell you these dragons have the magic to *shift* into elven form. They have two legs and arms and are elf size."

His mate blew out a breath. "Thank god. I was really worried for a minute."

He squeezed her to him again. Joy overflowed

in him that she hadn't run. He sprang to his feet and spun her around. She squealed and laughed. With her legs around his waist, he kissed her.

Earlier, Ryo had been correct when he said Zaos had big feet.

Those big feet tripped on themselves and a rock. And, yes, both he and his mate crashed into the water.

"Zaos," she surfaced, screaming. "I can't believe you...you—" she scraped hair from her face. Once he realized she wasn't furious, he snatched her up again and continued to spin them around. He set her on her feet and kissed the hell out of her.

Thank the Powers for cold water. If they kept this up, the pool would soon boil.

She giggled at him. "Why are you so happy?"

He held her shoulders in his big hands. "Because you are still here. You didn't abandon me, too."

He saw tears come to her eyes. No, no, no. Why was she crying?

She pushed onto her toes and wrapped her arms around his neck and squished him. "I'm so sorry you had to go through that heartache. I know how you feel. For the longest time, I felt abandoned by my mother. I didn't think she loved me after she and Dad divorced." She sniffled.

He pulled her arms down. "What?" He cupped his hand behind her head. "No one could ever not love you." Anger brewed in him. Anyone who upset his mate would pay. She was the most caring, nicest, warmest person he'd ever met. Though, he could be a bit biased.

She laughed. "It's okay. That was a long time ago when I was young. I'm fine now." She jumped up and down in the water and splashed around. "Oh my god! You're a freaking dragon. Lilah and Daphne would be shitting bricks if they knew this."

His magic instantly searched the area for others, finding no one. "Chelsea," he said, "if the elves know I'm part dragon, they will kill me."

She froze mid-splash. "No way."

"Dragons are our enemy. They've been the bane of our existence for centuries."

"Can't you live with the dragons, then?"

Anger erupted in his chest. "No." His statement was solid. "They didn't want me when I was a baby, they won't want me know. I fight to protect those who love and raised me."

She nodded. "Yes, I agree even if some of

them need an attitude adjustment." She waded toward the side toward a huge boulder sunk into the streambed. "This is cool." She brushed her hand over the rock. "Is this normal?"

He joined her to see what she'd found. The rock she stood beside had a section carved out. She dusted pebbles out of the indentation. "It looks like someone took a giant ice cream scooper and took out a middle chunk."

"I've seen several rocks with that feature. Don't know how it got there," he answered.

"It's so smooth, like something had sanded it." She hopped up and sat in the cut out. She leaned back to let the sun settle on her beautiful face. "Ahhh, this feels great. Just like in a hammock at the beach, except I'm fully dressed and need a piña colada."

He stepped closer to her, his fingers itching to take all those wet garments off her. "I can help with those clothes if they are bothering you."

She giggled. "I'd bet you would." Teasingly, she lifted the hem of her shirt. Despite the cold water, his dick thickened. Then her stomach made the loudest growl he'd ever heard. She yanked the shirt down, her face flushing. "Oops."

He laughed. "I guess we need to find you

something to eat." He noted the location of the sun. "It's time for the midday meal. We should get back."

She groaned, but dragged her legs over the side of the rock. He grabbed her around the waist and carried her to the grass. "Don't move," he said when he set her down. Her walking around in drenched material wouldn't do. With a twirl of his finger, both of their clothes were dry.

"That is cool," she said. "I so hate walking in wet underwear."

"I could find another way to help with that problem if you wanted."

She smacked his stomach with the back of her hand. "Yeah, I know. Race you back. Last one there has to eat all the nasty purple stuff."

CHAPTER EIGHTEEN

The path back to the caves was slipperier than Chelsea thought. She slowed coming around the first bend.

She was floored that Zaos was a dragon shifter. She didn't know such a thing existed. Of course, there were a lot of things she didn't know about this place. That explained why he was so much stronger and bigger than the others. King Gorwin made a wise decision in making Zaos his second-in-command.

But what surprised her about her mate was how vulnerable he was. He put himself out there, trusting that she would keep his secret. That meant a lot to her. Her ex kept a lot of secrets, and for good reason.

Her heart crumpled when he told her of his abandonment. No matter how big, tall, or strong you are, knowing you weren't wanted or loved was enough to crush any spirit. What he didn't realize, though, was that he'd proven his worth. If the birth father thought the boy wouldn't amount to much, he was fucking wrong and didn't deserve Zaos's love.

She agreed that the dragons lost a great opportunity to know a wonderful person, or elf, or elf dragon—elgon? Whatever he was. And she was extremely lucky to have found him, even if he would make a terrible dancer. They'd have to do something like skiing. He wouldn't even have to buy skis. She laughed.

"I hear you giggling up there," Zaos said behind her. Even though they were "racing," he stayed in back of her to make sure she was safe. He didn't have to say anything for her to know that's what he was doing. Otherwise, she was sure he'd be at the bottom now.

The trail led close to a cliff where she looked over and was awestruck by the view. Spread out far below, the mountain sloped gently into a valley that seemed filled with fire lilies. The forests were scattered into clusters with stretches of green between. Almost like roads had been there once and now were overgrown.

She stopped and took in the view. Zaos put an arm around her waist. "Beautiful, isn't it?"

He kissed the top of her head. "Yes, the valley is, too." She rolled her eyes at the so cliché comment. When she stepped back, the gravel under her running shoes slid and she lost her footing. She landed on her palms, breaking her fall. Zaos lifted her onto her feet, running his hands down her legs like he did this morning to check for injuries.

"I'm okay," she said. "Nothing broken." But the heels of her hands were scratched and bleeding from the rock. He gathered her wrists together then bent over and gently blew on them. She wondered what he was doing. When he straightened, she saw that her hands were healed. The gouges were gone and the scratched skin repaired.

"Oh my god." She stared up at him. "You did that, didn't you? You healed my hands."

"Yes, love," he said, "but it's another of my secrets you need to keep."

"Yeah, yeah, okay," she replied. "How did you do that? Do I have that magic?"

"You might. I don't know of any elves who can do it, though. There are stories of healers in our past, of course, back when we had large numbers of elves."

"You just breathed on it, right?" she asked. He nodded. "So freakin' cool. You're just so damn amazing." She tiptoed to kiss him, then took his hand to walk down together. "Why don't you want others to know about it?"

"It's kind of complicated, but if there's too many good things about you, others become jealous or suspicious and poke their nose where it doesn't belong."

"Ah," she said, "they might poke into your heritage and find out your *duality*."

"You got it. I use the healing as secretly as I can when others are injured. Sometime healing them enough to where they will survive without adverse effects, if it's that bad. My mom has taught me basic medical aid for battle wounds— wraps, coverings, how to stop bleeding. So I've become the go to guy if someone is hurt. It's usually just the children."

Chelsea stopped again and stared up at him. "You really care, don't you?"

His brow came up. "What do you mean?"

"You really are concerned about other's well-being. You want to make things better for every-one, not just yourself."

He shrugged a shoulder. "I guess. Doesn't everyone?"

"No," she said with certainty. "No, they don't." Her ex sure as hell wasn't worried about her feelings when he broke it off. "I'm hungry. Let's hurry."

Reaching the wooded area, she noted how many fire lilies covered the ground. They were stunning with the tendrils fluttering, looking so much like a small campfire. A hundred tiny camp-fires glowed all the way down.

"Do you use the fire lilies to heal, too?"

"You know about that?" he said, surprise in his voice.

"When I was in the village, one of the chil-dren stepped on something and became deathly sick in minutes. They had her drink water with a fire lily ground up in it. I guess it cured her." She wasn't positive since she hadn't seen the outcome.

"Yes, we use it in the same way. It does things I can't."

"They must be powerful, then." She recalled the story Ryllea told her and her cousins about the dragon queen dying and being buried. There was no shortage of the plant around here. They seemed to be everywhere.

Finally entering the cave, Zaos led her to the throne room where others gathered for the midday meal. King Gorwin came in from a side room and stood over a large area of dirt thinly spread on the floor. She hadn't noticed it there earlier.

He raised his hands and closed his eyes. On the floor, green leaves sprouted from nothing and grew into food she recognized from her meal that morning. More and more matured until the entire area was filled with food stuffs, including the purple thing she didn't like.

When the king lowered his arms, he looked exhausted and schlepped through the door he came out of.

"Is he going to be okay?" she whispered.

Zaos sighed. "He will after he rests. It takes a lot of magic to create the food we need."

"Good to know it's organic," she replied. All the items she would classify as vegetables and fruits. Broccoli lookalikes, carrots, potatoes, apples and oranges. No meat. That was interesting.

They sat at a long table with everyone else.

Glances, looks, and out-right stares came from those around her. All men. She recalled Hycis saying there were few women. She wasn't kidding. Most of the men were dressed in leather and what looked to be fighting attire, same as Zaos.

He conjured a fork and spoon for her while others simply ate with their hands. The food was really good. Tastes were different than she was used to. Most stuff she ate at home was so processed, she wondered how she was still alive.

"You know," she whispered to Zaos, "when I was at the village, one of the elder ladies went on about how dishonorable it was to use magic for simple things. And they had a ton of people bringing in baskets of food. And the chairs were made from tree roots. Oh my god, it was so cool. Then Tylen stood before everyone and—"

Zaos's hand slammed on the table. All seated stared at him. A growl from him vibrated her spoon next to her plate.

"If you are disgusted with us being dishonorable and weak, I suggest you leave." His nose flared when he breathed in.

She was gobsmacked. He was yelling at her. After all they shared and told each other and now he was having a freaking cow about the light elves?

"If we aren't good enough for you, go back to your high and mighty village."

She stood. "Did I say one word about how you do things?" Her leg pushed back her chair and she walked out.

"Chelsea," he called to her.

She spun around to face the eating room, everyone staring, some with their mouths open. "I'm following your advice and leaving."

He stood from the table. "Chelsea."

"Do not follow me. Or I will also leave *you*."

CHAPTER NINETEEN

The pain that shadowed Zaos's eyes from her threat to leave him cut through her, but dammit, he pissed her off. She hurried away from the dining area and quickly broke into a run. She needed to get out of here. Needed fresh air. Problem was she had no clue how to get to the damn entrance.

How dare he raise his voice at her. Adults were not supposed to yell. When adults got angry, they took a deep breath and realized the other person was entitled to their own opinion. And just because opinions clashed didn't mean either side was wrong. Just different.

But she didn't know what they disagreed on. What made him mad? Didn't he say he wasn't good enough? Where the hell had that come from? She didn't understand any of this. A lump began in her throat.

When she heard a baby, she realized she was close to the nursery. She headed in that direction. Inside the room, Hycis stood, burping an infant. When she saw Chelsea, she put the baby in a crib.

"What is wrong, daughter?" The woman took her into a hug. That bit of affection hit her in the heart. Her stepmother never warmed up to her when she was growing up. She never had the mother-daughter bond, never had anyone to go to with problems. And god forbid anyone hug or show love for each other in the home.

This display of care from a woman who'd only known her for an hour meant so much. Add that to the fact she somehow disappointed Zaos, and there was no stopping the tears. Fuck! She *hated* crying. Hycis held her and rocked like she did with the infant in her arms. No words, just a show of support and tenderness.

When she came to the hiccup stage, Chelsea pulled away, feeling stupid. She wasn't a child to cry when things didn't go her way. She couldn't meet the elf's eyes, afraid of what she might think.

Hycis guided her to the same chair she sat in

earlier and poured her a glass of water. Zaos's mother asked, "Do you know why we cry?" Chelsea shook her head, taking the cup of water in hand so she didn't have to look up. "It is because we love. We care. Crying means this person matters to you. Never be ashamed of your tears. It is how we show we cherish each other."

Hycis was right. She did care for Zaos. She did care what he thought and how he felt. And knowing that she said something to hurt him devastated her.

His mother continued. "It is when you do not cry that you know a problem looms." She laid a hand on Chelsea's arm. "Now, tell me, what did my son do?"

A laugh burst out of her with a hiccup. "How do you know it has to do with him?"

The woman smiled. "I know my son. I was waiting for him to say or do something that would upset you. I was hoping he'd make it past midday meal, but obviously not."

Chelsea grunted and sniffled. "This is my first time to your planet. I arrived with my cousins to visit my sister in the village." She saw the questions in Hycis's eyes. "I'm a human from Earth, but I recycle, drive an electric car, and use paper instead of plastic. So, please don't think bad of me just because our planet is in pathetic shape." Chelsea was surprised the woman didn't react at all to her being from Earth.

She asked, "What brought you to the village?"

"My half-sister is the new queen. We came to visit her." When Hycis nodded, Chelsea continued with her long-winded answer. "So, anyway, I'd just learned this morning about magic and how you're not supposed to use it for simple tasks and how tree limbs came out of the ground to make chairs for the tables and—"

Hycis lifted a hand and sat back in her seat. "I understand now, daughter." The elf sighed and looked at her. "Has my son told you about his birth parents?" Chelsea nodded. "Then I will speak of the part he didn't tell you."

What? He hadn't told her the whole story? Then he didn't trust her.

"This part of his story he does not know because he refuses to see it as a male."

Oh, never mind. She shouldn't judge without knowing all the facts. How many times had Grandmom told her that?

"Zaos was given to my husband for us to raise as our own. His feeling of abandonment runs deeply. He blames himself for not being good enough, worthy enough, for his father to want him."

"That's crazy," Chelsea said, nearly coming out of her chair. "He was a baby."

Hycis nodded. "Yes, I've told him over and over, but he is stubborn and believes his parents tell him non-truths because we love him." Both ladies shook their heads. "When you mentioned the light elves and their strong magic and 'honorable' living, he sees himself as inferior, not worthy of what he deserves."

"No," Chelsea said, "that's not what I meant."

"Of course not, daughter. Let me tell you about our history so you understand how he thinks."

Chelsea sighed. "That would be good. I can't believe he thinks of himself as unworthy."

Hycis began her story. "Eons ago, the dark elves, and dragons, lived in forests like the light elves. Our power was equal to theirs also. We grew our own food, sewed our own clothes, and lived honorably by our magic.

"When a power-greedy warlock wanted to sap our magic for himself and rule our land, we fought him. The battle was long and hard for he was very powerful from taking other creatures' power. When one of our arrows penetrated his shield, we thought it was over and life would return to normal."

Chelsea commented, "But it didn't, did it? It never does."

"As the warlock lay bleeding out, he cursed the dirt we lived on saying that if he could not control the land and those on it, nobody would. His blood poisoned the ground, making it sick, unable to grow food, and the forests died. We had no choice but to leave our homes."

"Oh my gosh," Chelsea said. "I couldn't imagine having to give up everything I had and starting over."

"Yes, we moved to where the ground was healthy and recreated our homes in the trees and our lives. Then the first storm came."

Just the way Hycis said the word *storm* gave her an ill feeling.

"After it had passed, everything was destroyed. Our homes were in shambles, food destroyed, and many of our own were dead. Only those who found shelter from the rain were uninjured."

Chelsea had no words to say. Images of California communities devastated by wildfires came to mind. Nothing but ashes left behind. "Is that why you moved into the caves?"

The elf nodded. "It was the only place we had to go. And over time, we lost our connection to the natural world. Little to no sun, no fresh air, no plants except for the little time we spend outside. Our abilities dwindled with the loss of the magic that had been around us constantly. Now, we have very little power compared to what we had and what the light elves still have. And we are forced to use magic for everything since we cannot grow food due to storms or have access to the resources we once did."

Chelsea had to know: "So, do you continue to get less powerful even now?"

"Yes, and that is one reason Zaos sees himself as lesser. He cannot do what the light elves can. We are no longer able to live honorably."

"But that's just as crazy as him thinking he was the problem with his father. It wasn't his fault. He had no control over any of it," she said. Hycis nodded in agreement.

Chelsea couldn't sit any longer and paced. Shit. She wanted to pull her hair out at his dumb self-imposed duty to take responsibility. She'd have to kick some sense into the man to get him to understand he has no say about what the Fates have decided. But she fully got where he was coming from now. Even if it was illogical.

"Thank you, Hycis. I understand now," she said.

"I knew you would. Give him time to adjust to having a life partner. He's been alone for so long among rough males."

The two exchanged another hug then Chelsea went in search of Zaos. But before she reached the busy hallways, Tel came around the corner.

Her heart nearly choked her, but she played it cool. As cool as someone ready to shit their pants could. Neither halted in their progress toward each other. His sneer unnerved her. What were the chances of him planting a knife in her back as soon as he passed? When he approached, she stepped aside and motioned him on by.

The prick stopped right in front of her, much too closely. She jammed her hand against his chest and straightened her arm. "You're in my personal space."

Tel's brows lifted. "Personal space?"

"Yes," she said. "If I can touch you, you're too close."

"Ah, seems Zaos has been in your personal

space. How's the fucking coming along? You've only got three days."

"That's none of your business," she said.

"It is if in three days you aren't stuffed with a little dwarf shit."

"Besides fucking my brains out, Tel, what do you want me for?"

The oily grin that spread across his face made her want to throw up. "I don't want you, female."

That didn't make sense. "Then why did you come to the king to claim me?" she asked.

"Because I didn't want him to have you." *Him* meaning Zaos, she was sure.

"Wait a minute." She shook her head. "You only want me because Zaos does?"

A growl from him tingled her hand still on his chest. "That dwarf dick has everything handed to him. I've fought my entire life to get where I am. Now he wants you, and I will do what is necessary to ensure he doesn't get what he wants."

"Well, I can assure you that you will never have me."

He pushed forward forcing her arm to bend. His face came within inches of hers. "Be assured that I don't need to have you for him not to."

CHAPTER TWENTY

Zaos stood by the dining table while everyone watched him fuck up with his mate. He stuffed a couple rolls into his pocket then stomped out after her. In the cave hall, he heard his father call to him from the table. *Shit*. He didn't need another confrontation.

"Come with me," his dad said as he exited the room. For some reason, the elder wasn't happy either. Dragon shit. He fisted his hands to keep from lashing out with anger. When they reached a secluded area, his father stopped and crossed his arms over his chest. With a scowl, the man said nothing.

Zaos paced, gritting his teeth. He knew he did that all wrong, but what if she found out he wasn't worthy of her, that he was a fraud? What would happen when she found someone better than him? Better that she left now so he could begin the grieving process.

His father's silence irritated him more. "Just tell me how to fix it!" he shouted. His dad's stiffened stance told him he'd gone too far. Fuck!

His father said, "I'll let it go this time because you need to find and apologize to your mate. What did you do wrong?"

"I don't know." He turned to pace the other direction. "I don't know."

"Have you forgotten where your mate is from?"

"No," he spouted.

"Did you not learn anything while you were there?"

"Of course, I learned," he ground out, "I was there for a hundred years."

"Then why are you doubting yourself?"

Zaos laid his forehead against the stone wall. "I don't know."

"Stop acting so simple-minded, Zaos. We did not raise you that way." His father's voice rang with frustration. How did the older elf think he felt?

He turned his back to the wall and slid down to sit, elbows on his bent knees. "I can't be good enough for her, Dad. She'll find a light elf so much better than me."

"Are you mocking the Powers That Be or the Fates?" His father leaned against the other wall.

"Of course not."

"Then why do you insist they put you with the wrong mate?"

He'd never said that. "She's not the wrong mate. Mates are supposed to be perfect for one another."

"Yes, they are. If you claim you are not good enough, then you say you're with the wrong mate. In your mate's eyes, you are more than good. You are perfect."

"Yeah, but—"

"And the witch?" Dad continued. "Do you want to tell her she is wrong."

"I'm not stupid, Dad. She'll turn me into a gecko." His dad didn't know what a little lizard was called so the joke was lost.

His dad huffed. "Let me put it this way then. Do you love her?" Both he and his dragon nodded. "Then if you don't become her mate, Tel has a chance to take her from you."

Zaos barged to his feet, his dragon nearly taking over. "No one else will touch her. She's mine." He barely recognized his own words through the growl.

His dad smiled. "That's more like it. Now start acting like the mate she deserves. Show her no one is better than you. Prove to her who you can be and will be for her."

Yes, yes, yes. He could do this. "Thanks, Dad. I have to find her and apologize for having my head up my ass." His father's eyes widened. "It's one of their sayings, Dad. Don't freak out on me here. Gotta go."

Zaos followed her scent in a twisted trail. It didn't dawn on him until now that she had no clue where she was going yet. Shit. How stupid could he be?

Then he picked up Tel's stink.

His dragon kicked his ass into overdrive. He delved deeper into the caves until he heard voices. He came around a corner to see Tel hit the wall on the other side of the hall from Chelsea. Tel's name ripped from his throat. The elf speared him with a look of suspicion. Zaos swallowed his dragon.

Chelsea ran to him and he took her into his

arms, staring down the bastard elf over her head. Tel walked away, but Zaos was sure the final showdown was yet to come.

He kissed his mate's hair. "I'm sorry, my love—"

"I'm sorry, too. There's so much I don't understand about you and this place. I didn't mean it when I said I'd leave you. I was just angry."

He leaned down, lips to her ear, hand tangled in her hair to hold her against him. "No matter what comes out of my stupid-ass mouth, know that I never want you to leave. You are my mate. I love you and will not live without you."

He'd come this far with his vulnerability, might as well go all the way. "I need you to teach me how to love you like you need. I want to be everything you want. I'm a battle-hewn male, rough on the edges. Not the least worthy of you, but I'm not letting you go. Tell me what I have to do to show you how much I care. I don't know how to do it on my own."

There. He'd said it. If she wanted to hurt him, she could cut his heart out and leave him to die right here, right now.

"I can do that," she mumbled where he smashed her face against his shoulder.

He loosened his grip. "Sorry."

She sniffed. "In return, I need you to help me understand you. You're a mystery to me, and I don't want to say anything that will make me doubt how much I care for you already."

"You've got a deal." He grinned, knowing he might get slapped for this, but, "Usually, when mates have a fight, they make up with sex afterward."

She patted his cheek hard a couple times. "You're funny. How about we go for a flight instead?"

His dragon perked up. That was perfect. She was perfect.

CHAPTER TWENTY-ONE

H and in hand, they ran to the waterfall where they'd find privacy.

Chelsea's heart soared high on love. After what he just said to her, that he wanted to be her everything, how could she not be over the top? That's not to say they wouldn't ever disagree again. But they understood where each of them stood.

They knew what they lacked and had asked each other for help. God, she had no idea what she was doing either in this relationship. It wasn't like she had role models to emulate. Neither of her father's marriages she would classify as a happily ever after.

But she knew together, they could do this. He

said he loved her. And she wanted to give her heart to him just as much. But a little piece of her mind held back.

"Let's do this," she said when they stood in the oasis far from any sign of life.

He leaned down and kissed her. A nice long kiss that warmed her girly parts. He breathed and cursed. She blushed, forgetting he could smell when her underwear was wet.

He stepped back and removed his leather gear with daggers and such. Then he moved on to sliding his shirt over his head. Oh hells bells. What a view. All those ripples she'd love to run her tongue down. Her pulse jumped. Then his hands moved to his waist.

"Um," she said "not that I don't like the show, but what are you doing?"

His grin turned wicked when unbuttoning his fly. Chelsea felt her eyes bug out. She probably looked stupid with her eyeballs about to fall out of her head. But dayum...

His pants skimmed down his hips, revealing that sexy V that pointed right where she wanted to be. Hmm. No boxers or briefs for her guy. Commando all the way baby. To be polite and because she was a bit shy, she turned away to give him privacy. Besides, she needed to catch her breath so she didn't look like a teen getting her first peek at a male body.

He walked up behind her and pressed all of himself, including *all* hard parts, against her backside. He whispered into her ear, "There will come a time when you'll not only watch me undress for you, but you'll be helping." He placed a hot kiss on her neck.

God help her. She wanted to strip down this second and ride him instead of his dragon.

She heard strange noises from his direction. Pops and cracks and a couple grunts. Then by her foot, almost like a snake, a tail grew longer and thicker until the smallest tip was as thick as her thigh. Her pulse pounded. This would be the most incredible experience in her life.

Slowly she turned, feasting her eyes on a white iridescent-scaled tail. Purples, blues, pinks, yellows flickered here and there depending how the sun shined on him. One color blending into another for a rainbow of shimmering light. He was as long as a semi-truck, including his tail.

She'd seen a million pictures of dragons in her lifetime. He resembled a dinosaur or a horse more than the snake-looking ones. He sat tall and proud with his neck stretched high. When her eyes finally roamed to his head, he winked at her. How could such a small gesture on a large creature be so sensual?

He lay on the ground for her to climb on. She stood next to his shoulder and realized even when he lay flat, he was too high for her to get on. Oh boy, this was going to be a problem. She needed to find the lowest spot on his body to climb onto then make her way to his back. And that would be...his tail or snout.

She headed for the tail. Stepping over the bottom portion, she straddled the scale-covered muscle looking for a way to climb up. There was nothing to grab onto and the hard covering felt slick like ice on a pond. Shit, this wasn't going to work.

She jogged to his head which was the size of car. "Uh, Zaos, love, the only way I can get on is by climbing up your face. Since my legs aren't as long as a giraffe, I'll need to crawl up your nose."

A screech came out of his mouth along with a stream of fire. She threw herself backward to not be roasted and sat panting on the grass. Something wasn't right with what just happened. She felt no heat. "Were you laughing at me?"

His head bobbed.

She moved closer to his mouth. "Can you do that again? Not the screech part, just the fire." He shook his head. "Come on, just a little." His head shook again, and his body seemed to slump as he lay. She sighed. "Zaos, I am your mate. I love everything about you. Even those things you don't like about yourself. They are a part of you, good or bad in your mind. I won't think any less of you because something about you isn't perfect.

"Hell, you're going to find a shitload of things about me that aren't perfect. And I can accept that because there's nothing I can do about it. But if you tell my sister I read her diary when we were kids, I will so hang you by your nuts, courtesy of Ryo."

A grunt sounded in his throat. She stomped to his mouth and pulled up his lip. "Damn, you've got big teeth."

His nose nudged her to the side and he blew out a small flame. She stuck her hand out and felt warmth, but no burning heat. His fire wasn't deadly. "Ah," she said, "you see that as a flaw. No frying with the blowtorch. Who cares?"

She stepped on his lip which boosted her high enough to get her leg up and over his snout. Just like getting on the hood of a car. Not that she'd done that much. "Where do you keep all this when in elf form? Don't move." She shuffled forward and leaned against the flat space between his eyes, like lying against a windshield. From there, she stretched out to grab onto the top spike and pulled herself up.

The scales here were as slippery as those in the tail. She wasn't confident about holding on while they were ten thousand feet in the air. "You know, Zaos, I'm not su—"

The jerk lifted his head and neck and she slid down, head first. Arms and legs splayed out as if making a snow angel, but on her stomach. She came to a stop halfway down his body, facing forward. That same shriek and outburst of fire came from him.

"Yeah," she hollered, "real funny. Just wait 'til I get your ass in roller skates. Then we'll see who's laughing." She shimmied up to his shoulder and looked over. She wasn't more than six or seven feet up, but she sucked at the high jump in school.

He moved a wing and she slid to the side. "Whoa." She grabbed a scale to not slide off. "Zaos, this isn't going to work." He grunted and bobbed his head. "How?" She returned to her spot by his neck where she could see over.

Something pressed on her legs, and she whipped around with a gasp. Zaos's beautiful plates had rearranged so they covered her shoes up to her thighs and locked her in. She wiggled around to test them.

"Huh, great idea. Let's go," she said.

With that, Zaos raised a bit, dipped down, then sprang upward while his wings drove themselves down. Almost passing out from the G-forces of the takeoff, she rested her chin on his shoulder and gasped at the incredible scene below.

CHAPTER TWENTY-TWO

C helsea had no words for the thrill she found soaring hundreds of feet above the ground. Her body felt as if she were flying solo.

Below, they passed over large fields as green as clover in the summer. Big open acreage with no smog or pollution or people crammed into small spaces. Vast forests spread for miles, nothing but trees forever. Animals that looked like deer, but could've been elephants for all she knew this high, roamed fields.

Zaos dipped low over a castle with many people milling around it. Behind it, a slope of grass led to a creek. Beautiful. He swept high into the sky, gliding on the air.

On the horizon, she saw something she couldn't make out. It spread wide, farther than she could see. The color shifted between greens and blues with occasional sparkles. Not until they were nearly over it did she realize it was an ocean.

The water was clearer than any she'd seen on earth, including the Bahamas. White ripples raced across the top, breaking into waves.

Zaos tucked his wings back and they plunged, the wind nearly ripping her hair out. An excited, adrenaline-filled shout rang from her throat. She felt so alive.

Being over the sea, Chelsea wondered if he planned on diving in. Should she remind him she couldn't breathe under water?

Preparing for a dunking, she took a big breath. But instead of going in, Zaos skimmed across the top of the water, casting out waves like a speeding boat. Mist sprayed up, cooling the effects of the hot sun.

Looking into the water, she saw many dark figures. Their silhouettes where humanoid. Well, they had two arms, a body, and a head. She couldn't see any lower. It appeared some of the water dwellers looked up at them. She waved and they waved back. She gasped; they were intelligent beings. Holy shit, mer-people? They were real!

Tipping his nose up, Zaos took them to an astounding height. A quarter of the globe spread below. Stunning blues and greens. All pure and clean with no black air or massive trash piles.

A patch of cream contrasted harshly against the green surrounding it. Judging the size, she thought it was about the same as Manhattan island. No green or trees anywhere. The place was dead. She'd asked Zaos later about it.

A mountain range seemed to go on forever, splitting the planet into halves. She laid her head on his shoulder and breathed it all in.

Slowly, they wound down, down, down, until she saw the waterfall oasis. Zaos floated over the open grassy area and settled gently on all fours. The scales holding her loosened and she slid off to the side.

On a natural high, Chelsea spun around with her arms out. What an amazing feeling. When she heard Zaos laughing, she ran straight for him, jumping and wrapping her legs around his waist. He barely moved from her impact.

Holding tightly, she laid a big one on him with her crazy elation. Yeah, the joy quickly morphed into desire. She couldn't help it. He was naked with all those yummy muscles for her to see. She moaned when he deepened the kiss, pulling her tighter against his chest. "Zao's, I need you please."

His answer was a growl and he turned, never breaking the kiss and walked a few steps away from the waterfall. Gently she felt him lay her down and she locked her ankles around his back. She didn't want him stepping away. She needed to feel his body against her, inside of hers.

CHAPTER TWENTY-THREE

"You're wearing too many clothes, my love."

Chelsea laughed and sat up, gripping the hem of her shirt and pulling it overhead. She could feel the heat from his gaze as it traveled across her skin. She shivered and laid back down. She wasn't going to hide from him.

"You're stunning and I'm going to worship every inch of your body." Zaos leaned down and blew hot air across her nipple. Even her white sturdy bra couldn't keep her from shivering. He grinned up at her and then moved to the other breast and blew more hot air.

Chelsea arched her back, bringing her breasts closer to his mouth. She moaned hoping he would take the hint but he chuckled. "Hmm, I'm in charge right now, I will set the pace and you will lay there and take it. Any questions my love?"

She shook her head, this was a side of him she hadn't expected but he was second in command. He couldn't have gotten there without being Alpha in his own right. Damned if it didn't make her panties melt either way. "Zaos paused and smiled, "you like that, don't you. Good, there's plenty more where that came from."

Chelsea felt a cool draft across the top of her thighs and realized she was naked from the waist down. She had no idea when he removed her pants but she was glad he had when she felt his hard cock press against her lips. "Yes, please!"

"Oh no, that too easy. I'm going to play a bit more before I take you." Chelsea groaned and sat up, then reached back to unhook her bra. Two could play at this game, she chuckled when she saw he was tracking her every move. She slowly slid the straps down her arms but kept the cups around her breasts. "Do you like what you see?"

"Move your hands and now." Zaos growly voice sent tingles along Chelsea's nerves and she shivered.

"Only because you asked nicely." She dropped

her hands and letting the cups fall away from her body. She slowly lowered herself back to the lush grass and waited to see what his next move would be.

Zaos sat back on his heels and stared at her for a moment. "You are the most stunning woman I've ever seen. The fates blessed me when they made you my mate."

He tenderly reached out and rand his hand down her neck, across her breastbone and around the curve of her breast. His fingers grazed across the nipple and she shivered again. "Are you cold my love?"

Chelsea narrowed her eyes and reached up and ran her hand across his thigh and around to his cock. "I'm warming up nicely." A wicked glint entered his yees and he scooted back to straddle her knees. "I didn't say you could touch me yet. I told you I was playing and you must take it all."

Chelsea let her hand drop to the ground by her hip and waited to see what he would do next.

He leaned down and licked her thigh, then his hot tongue traveled across her belly and he swirled it in her belly button. "Nothing could ever taste as good or as sweet as your skin."

Chelsea gasped as heat filled her and she felt

wetness dripping down her thighs. He continued his way up her body and everywhere he touched, goosebumps broke out. She clenched her hands into the grass and writhed under him. When he finally reached her breast again, her belly clenched and she panted. Waiting for him to finally take her nipple into his mouth.

He blew on her nipple again and then licked his way up to her neck and then started kissing his way to her mouth. She turned her head to kiss him fully and he chuckled and started kissing his way back down her neck. This time he sucked her nipple into his mouth and she arched her back moaning louder.

"Please Zaos, stop teasing me." Chelsea ran her hands down his back and lightly scratched at him. She needed him to feel how desperate she was.

With a pop, he pulled his mouth off her breast and kissed his way down to her belly, for a moment he laid his cheek against her and she ran her hands through his hair. Then he gently kissed her and moved lower, spreading her thighs and glancing up at her.

"Are you ready?" With a smirk, he looked back down and flicked her clit with his tongue.

She shot up into a sitting position and grabbed his head. He did it again, and she swayed a little. His right hand ran up the outside of her leg to her stomach and up between her breasts. He gently pushed her so she laid spread out on the grass again.

She lost track of time as he assaulted her senses with lust, each swipe of his tongue sent her body into spasms, after a few more swipes he gently inserted a finger and started thrusting in and out of her wet pussy. "Dammit, Zaos." She moaned and arched her back, then reached down to tug on his hair.

"Not yet." Zaos looked up at her but didn't remove his tongue from her clit and he added a second finger. "I want you unable to talk, I was the only sounds coming out of your mouth are grunts and moans. Then and only then will I line my cock up with you and fill your body over and over until you scream out my name."

He thrust his fingers in and out over and over and each time her walls clenched a bit more. Just when she thought she would explode he relented and stopped for a moment. Then he slowly licked her from her ass to her clit and then sucked it into his mouth. She exploded into a million stars and screamed. She could hear the sound but it sounded as if it came from a great distance away.

A few minutes later she came back to herself and felt his hands running up and down her body. When she made eye contact he smiled and lined up his cock with her opening and slowly pushed in. "Stay with me love."

Chelsea stared into his eyes and together they climaxed, connected body and soul.

CHAPTER TWENTY-FOUR

Evening meal passed much quieter and happier than the midday meal had. Zaos hated that all the men and the few women stared at her, but she was the shiny new toy nobody knew anything about. Plus, she was with him, who'd never shown much interest in the females before.

He was sure she was itching to ask questions. After their lovemaking session—a thrill at the memory of it rushed to his cock. Dragon shit— they hurried back to catch the available food. The sexy woman sat where their legs touched. He wanted so much more again, and again, and again.

Which brought to mind her staying quiet

around the men. He also wanted to discuss what she told the king about helping them. He needed to talk her out of doing anything. No telling what could happen, including her getting killed.

After eating, he walked them to his room. Seeing that the bed was much too tempting for them to sit on, he conjured a big round chaise-like chair they could share and talk. He sat and stretched his legs out and his mate snuggled into him.

"What an incredible day," Chelsea said, rubbing her hand over his chest. "So much has happened. My brain feels overwhelmed."

"You don't feel like talking about anything then?" he asked. Everything could wait until tomorrow.

She frowned. "I want to know about the big patch of dirt. You could plant trees and grow a vast forest and live there. That would solve almost all your problems. You'd still have the population issue, but with no cave-ins, at least your people are safe."

"That would be nice," he said, "but there is a reason we haven't done that."

"I figured something was up with it," she said.

"A long time ago, that's where we used to live, and it was covered by lush forests and streams of fresh water. Hundreds of species of plants and small creatures thrived. The tall trees with their large leaves kept most of the sun from the ground, just enough to keep the air warm and ground moist."

"Sounds like the movie *Avatar*," she said.

"Haven't seen that one, so I'll take your word on it."

"Ha," she replied, "you're funny."

"I know I am love." He kissed her forehead. "Our homes were in the trees, made from branches and vines configuring around our needs to let the breeze flutter through all day. In sunny sections of flat land, we had huge areas to grow our food.

"Some of the growers were trying out ideas to blend items into new foods. Some things worked, some didn't." He sighed. "Back then, everything was nearly perfect, which was probably why it had to come to an end."

"Wait," she said. "Is this where the wizard cursed the ground with his blood?"

"Yes, how do you know that?" he asked.

"Your mother told me about it. She said he

poisoned he dirt. Has no one figured out how to *unpoison* it?"

"No, many have tried with no success. The most powerful have said it will take several things together to reclaim the land."

"Wow," she said, "what a waste."

"Agreed."

"Is there a way to communicate with the dragons?"

He smiled, finding her bouncing thoughts funny. "They have elven forms."

"Oh, right. I forgot," she said. "I need to talk with them tomorrow."

He fidgeted on the cushion. "I don't want to see or talk to them." Anger and hate rolled through him when thinking of the dragons and how they abandoned him. He didn't think he'd be able to talk civilly with them.

Chelsea scooted off the chair. "Did I say 'you'? No. I said me." She held her hand out. "Are you coming with me to tell the king?"

Disgruntled, he rose and took her hand. He definitely wasn't happy with this. He didn't want to let her go, but who was he to stop her? *Her* mate, *that's who*. He hushed his dragon side.

He deactivated the magic field that separated

his room from those passing by in the hallway and walked her out. Reaching the throne room, he asked to see if the king was available. The past several summers the king had returned to his room earlier and earlier. Without a mate, his spirit was getting tired. He became grumpier and more irritable without someone to share his heart with.

Zaos feared the king may soon step down and pass everything on to his chosen heir—himself. The Powers! He didn't want to rule over a land with so many problems.

King Gorwin was on the throne, so he walked Chelsea before the royal, then took his place at the side of the throne.

"Hi, King Gorwin," Chelsea said. Zaos could tell she was a bit nervous, but so were elves who'd been around for hundreds of summers when it came to talking with the king. "I've been speaking with Zaos about what I can do to help with the challenges you face—"

The king laughed. "*Challenges*," he said. "You have a nice way of putting things, young one."

She rolled her eyes. "Yeah, blame it on the times I live in. Anyway, tomorrow, I'm going to talk with the dragons to—"

"No. I forbid you from going," the king said.

Oh, dwarf shit. Zaos cringed as his mate's face turned red and her eyes narrowed. This was not good.

"Should I remind you, elven king," she said slowly, "I am a guest here, not a royal subject. I will do as I please."

The king leaned forward in his golden monstrosity. "You are in my land, elf, and you will do as I say."

Her hands fisted and Zaos wasn't sure if she would pummel the ruler or not. He wasn't about to give her that chance. "Milord," he said, "I will go with her if you so desire."

The king sat back and looked over his shoulder at Zaos. "If you keep her safe, then she may go." He watched his mate deflate. Some.

"Thank you, My King." With that, Zaos hurried forward, grabbed her hand and exited before she came up with some retort.

On the way back to his room, she said, "I thought you didn't want to go."

"I don't," he said.

She pulled on his hand to make him stop in the passageway. "Then why did you volunteer to go with me?"

He sighed and looked away. "Because this is

important to you. If the king allows you to go only if I am there to guard you, then I'll do that."

Her eyes turned glassy. "You'd do it for me?" Her hand brushed the side of his face. Her scent filled him, her soft touch invigorating.

"Of course," he whispered. "I'd do anything for you."

She raised onto her toes and kissed him. Not a quick peck, but a deep, desirous kiss. He backed her against the cave wall and pressed into her. She groaned when his hard cock rubbed on her mound. Fuck, he wanted her again, and again, and again. He'd never get enough of her.

With her ankles locked behind his back, he carried her to his room, activating the invisible divider, and laid her on the bed. "How are your ribs?" he asked. Before he made love to her again, this time he'd do the gentlemanly thing and make sure she was healthy. Fuck, he was such a savage.

She blinked up at him. "Can you heal bones like you did my scrapes?"

That was a good question. "I'm not sure. I can't really breathe on them directly." He lifted his hands toward her midsection then stopped.

"Umm, can I touch...your sides?"

Chelsea giggled and raised her shirt to the

bottom of her bra. Just this small piece of skin drove him insane. He wanted so much more than just to feel her.

He dropped his magic around her and she had no reaction. His hands lay on her flesh and electric shocks stung him. He rubbed up and down, feeling her bones too easily. She was too thin. He continued to brush his hands down to her waistband and placed a kiss in the dip of her side. Then he kissed his way up her stomach.

When he looked up at her, she was sound asleep, as beautiful as an angel. Yes, he loved this woman and would go wherever she went. Even if that was back to her planet.

CHAPTER TWENTY-FIVE

The next morning, Chelsea snuggled into her warm sheets. Zaos's smell encircled her. She took a deep breath then realized she'd fallen asleep in Zaos's room. Her eyes popped open to see the place dimly lit.

"Good morning, love." Zaos sat stretched out on the large barrel chair. "How are you feeling?"

She sat up, finger-combing her hair. She was sure she had the worst case of bed head the world had seen. "What time is it?" she asked.

"The break fast meal is over, but there is still a lot of time before midday," he replied.

Chelsea tossed off the covers. "You guys really need to adopt hours and minutes."

Zaos stood and carried a tray of food to her.

He replied, "There is no reason. We live by nature and have little need for such restrictions."

She hadn't thought about that—how much of her life was ruled by the clock. She got up at a certain time, worked so many hours, had to be to the store before it closed at a certain time. Her entire life was tied to the twenty-four hours between sunrises.

She took the tray he offered and scooted up the bed to lean against the wall. "Thank you for saving breakfast for me. I usually don't eat in the morning, but I'm starving today."

"As soon as you are ready, we can leave for the dragon's domain."

She thought he sounded a little different this morning and now realized why. "Zaos, I'll be fine going on my own. The dragons have nothing against me so they won't hurt me."

"Are you certain of that?" he asked.

Well, no, she wasn't, but there was no logical reason for them to attack her. "I'm not a dark elf if that makes a difference."

He sighed. "I don't know if it will or not. The dragons haven't bothered us except by indirectly killing us through cave-ins in summers. But I am not letting my mate walk into enemy territory—

adversary or not—by herself. You know I can't live without you, right?"

Words failed her at the pain she felt in his voice. He was serious. This wasn't just when a romantic said *I can't live without you*. Zaos meant it. She had to consider that in all she did. In a way, she was responsible for his life. Talk about a heavy burden. Damn.

After a few more bites of a green sweet thing, she was ready. "Let's get this over with." It killed her that Zaos wasn't his smiling, happy self. She'd come to like that he was settled in his life and knew where he fit in society. She was still working on that.

She followed him out of the cave and up a trail through the trees.

"How far do we have to go before we get there?"

"Not far, just to the top edge of the forest," he answered.

Not far? That didn't make sense. If they were that close, wouldn't she have seen them by now? She saw a lot of the mountain when they went to the waterfall. She never gave it much thought since so much was going on yesterday.

About ten minutes later, Zaos stopped where

the forest came to an abrupt end. "That's their land?" she asked. A few trees stood within sight. But she could see to the top of the ridge, and there were no dragons on the mountainside. "I don't get it."

"Magic, love. They have many more people they can draw upon to make stronger magic. They hide their existence from others that way."

Okay, she'd just wait and see what she saw. He took her hand and held tightly.

He said, "Let me do the talking," then stepped forward.

Chelsea felt her insides wobble like a tall column of Jell-O. A tingly sensation almost tickled her entire body. Then her eyes didn't believe what they saw.

The mountainside was no longer made of sloping rock but a stack of stone platforms like different floors in an office building. The first floor was over their heads where people walked around doing whatever. This was a rock village built into the side of the mountain.

On the bottom most level, humanlike men appeared, carrying baskets filled with something. From there, others took the baskets and moved out of her sight. Even children existed. Many dragged long leaves along the ground, going someplace she couldn't see.

Then the ground shook, messing with her balance. But Zaos kept her from falling.

From both sides, fucking huge dragons closed in on them. They say that people imagine expressions on animals' faces, that they don't really feel what they show. But the pissed off-edness on these creatures' mugs were enough to scare the shit out of her. She was about ready to climb Zaos like a tree, and it wasn't for sex reasons.

He shouted, "We are here to speak with your king. We mean no harm." He lifted his arms to show he had no weapons. She couldn't imagine anything but a nuclear bomb affecting such massive beings.

The dragon lifted his head and roared. Chelsea was ready to shit her pants. She trembled, gripping Zaos's shirt. She tried to look as unaffected as possible, which she wasn't at all. A few moments later, another roar from high up caught her attention. The two dragons on each side of them shifted into humanoids the same size as Zaos. Which was still pretty damn big to her.

They dressed in beige robes that hung from their shoulders. She doubted they had anything on underneath. One of the men came to stand inches from Zaos's face. "Unbelievable," he said. He stepped back and glanced at Chelsea, not giving her much thought. She was fine with that.

"Follow me," the guard said. Zaos held her hand and led her behind their escort. She noted the other guard brought up the rear. She thought it weird they had no weapons. All the movies and books she read had guards always carrying spears and daggers. But if their magic was strong, what use was a sharp metal edge?

As they approached a misty, cloudlike place at one side of the platforms, a set of stairs appeared. They climbed into the gray fog. Looked like this morning, instead of running, she was doing stair steps.

When they came to the next level, another cloud formed, blocking their view of what was on the level. She saw people moving around but that was it. After a hundred or so steps, they stopped and went onto a grassy surface.

Again, she couldn't believe her eyes. The area was as big as the main section of the light elves' village. The space was empty, though, no sign of life until an old guy popped into view, running toward them. The guards bowed when he was closer. This dude wearing normal elf clothes was their king? He seemed more like her sister's mate Tylen than King Gorwin.

The man came to a screeching stop in front of Zaos. Chelsea notice the weathered look their king had. But the astonishment on his face made him look younger.

She looked at Zaos to see if he had a clue why the king was so excited. Seeing his brows drawn and a frown, she figured he didn't know what the hell was going on either.

The king stepped closer to her mate. Zaos could easily touch the man if he lifted his arm.

"Oh, the Powers That Be," the king said. "You look exactly like my mate, your mother."

CHAPTER TWENTY-SIX

O f all the things that could've happened venturing into the dragon's realm, being told he looked like his mother and facing his father wasn't anywhere even close to being on the list.

"Of course," the man went on, "you have manly features instead of her feminine ones."

Anger and heartache erupted inside Zaos's chest. He kept his balled hands at his side. This man who didn't want him, now looked happy to see him. Well, too bad. He should've thought about that before the man dumped him on an elf.

Chelsea must've figured out the same since she held tightly to him, keeping him from simply leaving without making a big scene. While the king stood speechless, Zaos ground his teeth together then looked away.

"I am Zaos of the dark elves. This is Chelsea. We are here to discuss solutions to the challenges existing between the dark elves and dragons."

The king's smile faded. Ha, that made Zaos feel better.

The elf stepped back. "I don't understand. You are my son—"

"No, I am not," he barked. "I am the son of Klaern and Hycis of the dark elves."

The man froze, horror on his face. "Y-you have been alive all these summers in the elves' caves?"

Now Zaos didn't understand. His father was the person who gave his infant son to Klaern. Well, the female actually handed over his infant self, but she was there in place of the father, right? Why was the ruler acting like he had no idea where he had been? Zaos met his eyes. They were glassy. He'd never seen a king cry. What was going on that brought such emotion to this man?

Chelsea leaned against him, keeping him sane. She said, "Let me get this straight." She pointed to the old man. "You are Zaos's birth father and you had no idea he's been with the elves? The story I heard was that you gave Zaos to a woman to give to Klaern because you didn't want the baby."

The man's hand went to his forehead. "What? I would've died for my son. Never would I give him away. Where did you hear such lies?"

Shock rolled through Zaos. He swayed on his feet, but his mate had him. His father hadn't wanted to give him up? Why would his mother lie, telling him the opposite?

"That's not important," his mate said. "Can we go somewhere more private and sit?"

The king shook his head. "Of course, I don't know what's wrong with me. I'm usually quite cordial. Follow me." He nodded to the guards and they left down the stairs. Chelsea tugged Zaos forward as his mind continued to whirl out of control.

Their expansive surroundings seemed normal with grass on the ground, flowers, insects, and clouds overhead. But he knew this was magic because the mountain did not have flat areas this big. But it was nice with the warm breeze.

At a small cottage, his father opened the door for them to enter. The place was cozy with a living space filled with places to sit. But the air held a sense of sadness. It felt heavy, weighed down with grief and loneliness. Much like his own room in the cave.

Chelsea and he sat while the king had beverages brought in. "Thank you," Chelsea said. "We appreciate your warm welcome."

The king stared at Zaos and said, "I am Larongar, leader of this clan of dragons."

A silent moment was upon them where nobody knew what to say. He certainly had no words yet. His mind was on sabbatical.

"So, King Larongar," Chelsea said, "Zaos and I are here to talk about the problems you are experiencing with the dark elves. We hope to find solutions for both sides. But, obviously, there's other things we should discuss first. We were told that Zaos was given up as an infant. I'm guessing that's not what happened."

"No, not at all." Larongar sat back, his hands shaking. "When you were ten sun cycles old, your mother took you to her favorite spot overlooking the vast waters. She was well inside dragon land and in no danger of intruding enemies.

"When she didn't show for evening meal, I knew something was very wrong. We searched for her and you for days. I never gave up, continuing after others took rest. Then three sun cycles later, your mother's body washed ashore."

Zaos watched as his father went from a happy, vibrant man to almost a ghost of a being.

"I was so bereft. A large part of myself died at that time. She was my mate, a beautiful dark elf meant for a dragon king."

"Did you find out what happened? Who killed her?" Chelsea asked.

Larongar shook his head. "We found no trace of anything out of the normal. It could've been an elf who made his way in. But I will never believe she meant to end herself and our son. She was a happy person who loved life." His chin dropped to his chest.

"What of the baby?" she asked.

The king sighed. "We assumed he perished alongside his mother. We never found his tiny body." He gestured at Zaos. "Now, it's obvious why."

Chelsea glance at him then turned to Larongar. "You never gave Zaos to the elves because you didn't want a baby?"

"Never!" His father's raised voice sent waves of hope through him. "I loved my son and mate with all my soul. When I lost them both that day, I planned on joining them in the great afterlife. But many of the dragons convinced me not to. They said they needed me."

Smiling at Zaos, his father said, "Now, I'm glad I did as they wished. But for many, many summers, I wished not to be in this world any longer. Only the babies kept me going. Knowing I had to secure their futures. Protect them."

He heard giggling and his eyes found a window with others peeking in. The king stood and shooed them away with promises of more information later.

When the king returned to his chair, Chelsea asked, "Was there anyone here who would've wanted her gone?"

Larongar shook his head and turned away. "No. None of which I am aware. Your mother was loved by everyone. She had a tremendous ability to heal the ill and injured." Zaos's body jerked with that revelation. "Creatures came from great distances to see her. She welcomed them all with open arms."

He finally could speak. "How did she heal?"

"She had what we called the Breath of Life. All she had to do was breathe on someone and their bodies became well again."

Zaos glanced at his mate. She had the same knowing look that he probably did. That answered one of the mysteries about himself. "I have that ability also," he said. "I've kept it to myself so others wouldn't be suspicious of me. I've used it secretly."

The king leaned forward and took Zaos's hand. "Then truly, you are my son."

CHAPTER TWENTY-SEVEN

Chelsea sat flabbergasted with the turn of events. This was better than fiction. A son, lost as an infant, comes back to meet his father, who he thought gave him up. God, it sounded like a Hallmark movie.

And to learn the story she and Zaos had been told wasn't true. She didn't think Hycis would flat out lie to her. There must be a mix in the story as the years went on. Like playing telephone where the sentence started as *Brad Pitt is the hottest babe*, and ended up with *bra mourns the bub*.

Damn, what a surprise. She wasn't worried about Zaos's quietness. She was sure he was reeling from the news. She needed to ask the questions he would if he was mentally capable. And some for herself.

She thought back to the king's comment on the babies. She wondered how many they had. The elves had so few, it was worrisome.

"How many newborns do you currently have?" she asked.

Larongar's face lit up. "Would like to see them? They are so precious."

Before she could tell him no in a polite way, they were magically whisked into a dark, chilled place with little light. The walls and floor were the same as the dark elves' cave. Why here?

"Where are we?" Zaos asked with a growl. Apparently, he wasn't thrilled with the *beam me up, Scotty* way of getting around. In the near distance, she heard a baby cry. She followed Larongar as he entered a very large room with over a dozen little ones. They ranged in age from newborn to a year old.

The ladies and men attending to the babes gasped and kneeled when the king entered.

"I apologize for the unannounced intrusion," Larongar said. "But I want to show our future to...guests."

Chelsea noticed the older dragons staring at

Zaos, wide-eyed. They must've recognized him from his resemblance to his mother.

"Do you have this many younglings every summer cycle?" Zaos asked.

"The number varies per mating season, but not by much," his father answered.

Wow, she thought, with this many additions, the population had to have grown immensely over the years. The exact opposite of the elves.

"Bringing the new lives into the community has put a strain on our resources. We continue to expand, having many dragons slumber much farther from the center than I'd like." Larongar tensed, tightening his hands 'til his knuckles were white. "They become vulnerable to attack by the dark elves who have no reason for such violence aimed toward us."

"Are you joking?" Zaos said. "We've lost many due to dragons burrowing under the ground and causing cave-ins. Women and children included."

The king frowned, brows down. "I don't understand. My dragons cause cave-ins? How? Where?"

Whoa. Chelsea realized they had a situation where not everyone was on the same page. She put her divorce mediator experience into gear.

"Larongar, we should speak privately about this."
She tilted her head slightly toward the adults
tending to the babies.

"Yes, I agree. But I want my battle leader to
hear this also." The king spun on his heel and
headed another direction through the underground location. She and Zaos followed. Not too
far ahead, sun shined into the opening. They
emerged on a different level than what they had
been on.

Chelsea wasn't sure what she was seeing.
People—dragons—raced around in virtual chaos.
Many came directly toward them, fear on their
faces. The king turned and stared into the distant
sky. "No."

She looked back to see what scared the king. It
looked like a storm was on its way with dark
clouds building.

"Dragon shit," Zaos said, then looked at her.
"Guess I need to find another curse word."

The king faced them. "Go into the nursey to
hide from the storm. The rest of the village will
come. We all wait in there."

"I will help gather the people," Zaos said,
pushing her toward the cave they just exited.
"Wait for me inside." He took off across the

area, helping others tie down things and whatever else.

She harrumphed. No way was she hiding from a little rain. She could help just as much as he did. And she had speed to use to her advantage.

Seeing the stairs in the mist they climbed earlier, she hurried down to the next level. People ran around here like they did above, so she continued down.

The next rocky platform had fewer people than the others. This site had more forest-like plants and trees. The ground was also churned up like they just filled in a huge circle in the ground. Here, they shoved goods into wallowed out holes in the ground and covered the top with stones and dirt.

Chelsea hollered, "Do you need any help?" One of the men glanced at her, but didn't say anything before he disappeared like he'd never been there. That disoriented her a bit and she fumbled down a step. Magic like that would take some getting used to.

Another of the men shifted into his dinosaur —uh, dragon—and dove head first into the broken-up dirt. She watched amazed as the animal went around and around, each circle moving the topsoil less. Which told her it was going deeper.

Oh, shit. Was that what Zaos meant when he said the dragons burrowed down to the bedrock that made up the caves? Many others did the same. The steps below where covered by the strange fog, so she hoped that no lower levels existed.

She was about to run up when she heard someone yelling. She headed inland to see what was happening. Someone might need help. And she was right. A female ran among the bushes, calling out a name.

"Can I help?" Chelsea asked.

The woman stared at her for a second. Chelsea was a stranger, yes, but she was here to assist.

"My daughter is missing. I cannot locate her."

"Where could she be? Close to here?" she asked. The woman nodded and shouted *Amerisa*.

Chelsea ran the area, hollering the same name. The trees and ground cover impossibly stretched out as if there were miles of forest here. But she saw from below there wasn't. Geesh, was that a mind blower or what?

The environment was the same as the woods around the caves, which included numerous fire lilies. She couldn't see the sky through the leaves high up, but the storm had been far off. She had a lot of time before the rain started.

The wind picked up, much stronger than she expected. While looking for the child, her brain recalled the story Hycis told her about the storm destroying their homes. Maybe this would be worse than just a rain shower.

In a patch of clover, she glimpsed a piece of red and headed that way. In the center lay a little girl sleeping. She didn't want to scare the girl so Chelsea hid behind a tree and hollered her name. The child woke and looked around.

"Hello, there," Chelsea said from behind the tree. She waited a moment then poked her head around the trunk. The girl startled, but didn't seem scared. "Hi," Chelsea said again. "Your mama is looking for you. You need to hurry back before the storm gets here."

The color drained from the child's face and she ran. Chelsea followed to make sure she made it back and because she wasn't sure herself how to get back. The girl called out to her mother and the two connected then promptly disappeared.

They must have magicked themselves to the underground nursey.

She hurried to the stairs. When she placed her foot on the step, the tread vanished and she fell to the ground. She slid several yards before she was able to jam her feet on stable rocks.

Around her, the platform levels were gone, as was the mist. She was surrounded by rocky, mountainous terrain lacking any plants or animals. Far to the side, she saw some trees, but not nearly the number that had been there. What the hell happened?

The wind whipped her hair around her face, stinging her cheeks. She tried to stand, but the force of the air nearly pushed her over, falling lower on the incline. Chelsea glanced at the sky. The storm was almost on them. Well, shit. Looked like she was going to get wet.

In the corner of her eye, she saw a movement that turned her head. In the forest over the caves, the tops of the trees burst into flames then the leaves crumbled into ash. More and more were doing the same thing.

It looked as if small bombs were going off, frying the small area around it. She wondered what caused that. As she watched, it seemed the bombs made their way across the forest in a linear fashion.

Then the ground on the mountain over there let off steam as if a natural hot water spring. Strange. She reminded herself she wasn't on Earth. Anything was possible here.

A bad feeling started settling in her stomach. She studied the rain and clouds and realized the rain was causing the leaves to burn to ash and the rocks to sizzle with smoke.

Oh, fuck. That wasn't just rain, but acid rain. And she had nowhere to take cover.

CHAPTER TWENTY-EIGHT

Zaos assisted those burying food, pottery, and goods. He had no idea why they were hiding such things. Why not just carry them inside shelter? He knew the rain would destroy anything it touched. Dissolve it down to nothing or burn it to ash.

After digging several holes, depositing contents, then refilling the remaining space, he noticed how everybody ran to the nursery. He was glad he had his mate stay there. He knew the cave would keep her safe.

When no others were outside except him and his father, they hurried to the shelter. The king quieted everyone and began their routine for when this occurred, starting with calming the children. There were so many of them. More than he had ever seen of the elves.

It was no wonder the amount of land the community needed just to sleep had expanded so much. The dragons thrived. And at the expense of the dark elves.

He looked around the crowd for his mate. The people were so diverse, it wasn't easy to spot her. There were redheads, dark brown and golden hair. Pale skin as well as brown and very dark mixed together.

When his heart began beating harder, he called out to her. She didn't respond. Quickly, he moved through the crowd, pushing others with more force than he intended. "Chelsea! Chelsea!"

He came to a woman with a little girl in a red top with leaves and pine needles stuck to her clothing. The woman asked, "Was she wearing strange men's clothes?"

Zaos almost answered no, then realized all the woman here wore some type of dress while men had on trousers. If any female was in pants, it would be his mate.

"Yes," he replied. "Where is she?" His eyes continued searching the area.

"She helped me find my child," the woman

said. *Wonderful*, Zaos thought. His mate was caring in that way, but it didn't help him find her. "No," she continued, "you don't understand. My daughter was lost in the lower level woods. The female found her sleeping."

"What?" Zaos nearly shouted. The female stepped back, fear in her eyes. "I am sorry for the harsh tone. But I can't find her now. Did she come back with you?"

"No. I didn't bring her. She is a stranger to me."

Fuck. He understood the reasoning for not wanting to have an unknown person around, but dammit, a storm was coming. Maybe she'd found shelter in another structure.

He hurried back to the front entrance and climbed the steps leading outside. "Son," his father called out, "stay in here. The rain will kill you."

"I know," he said as he picked up the pace, "and my mate is in it."

"I must recall the magic," the king said.

Zaos stopped. "You what?"

"I must take back the magic. Everything you've seen is created by combined power of the people. This cave is the only real place."

Zaos shook his head. "Are you telling me there will be no place for my mate to find shelter?"

His father's expression fell. "That is correct." The older man pushed him toward the opening. "Find her quickly, Zaos. Bring her here. Don't let my mate's fate be your mate's." His mother's death.

Zaos ran outside, yelling for Chelsea. The green grass and village around him disappeared, leaving him on blanched rock, stripped through the summers by the rain. The wind slapped against him, nearly knocking him down. He'd never experienced this part of a storm. He was always inside the caves like all the other sane elves.

Close behind him, he heard the exposed rock sizzling as the acid ate away the outer layers. Far below, the forest—his forest—was systematically being eradicated of life, turned to ash. Which would be his mate if he didn't find her.

Controlled panic racing through him, he yelled her name. She could be anywhere. The woman said the lower level, so he headed down the incline. He noted the circular areas where the ground had been lifted. Those were the dragons who dug deep under the soil for safety.

Could she be with one of them? She wouldn't be able to breathe if she were. He kept moving. The rain was gaining on him. The wind blew ash, his eyes stung and the tang settled in the back of his throat. He hollered her name, but choked before he got it all out.

He ran from the rain to the top of a hump in the mountainside where he could see farther. His sharp eyes surveyed the area below and above.

A sting on his arm sent pain screaming though him. A raindrop had fallen on his skin. He sprinted away, the clouds moving faster than he anticipated. Shit, at this rate, his mother's fate would be his own.

Then he saw her. She was but a speck moving across the desolate ground. Even with his elven speed, it would take time to reach her. Her speed was extremely fast. She must've been using her magic to amplify her running ability, the way she had when she and Ryo bumped into him exiting the smaller cave entrance yesterday.

He yelled for her, but she was too far away, plus the wind ate his voice. Another bite of pain hit his leg. Dwarf fuck! The only way he could outrun his death was to shift. He could get his mate then and find a place to hole up until the storm passed or died out.

The sparkling white dragon was more than happy to hold their mate and carry her off where they could mate. *No*, he told his other half. *We are not having sex while death is so close.*

His dragon took flight with a snort saying they'd see about that.

In a matter of seconds, they reached their little mate. He screeched so she would know he was coming. She looked over her shoulder then came to a sliding stop. He heard his name from her sweet lips.

His body relaxed a bit and he breathed which he'd forgotten to do since he shifted. He landed and lowered his neck to the ground. Like a pro, she ran along his snout and dove for the top of his head, sliding down his neck onto his back.

He moved his scales to cover her, holding her to him. With a short squawk as a warning, he jumped up with a powerful down thrust of his wings. Now the trick was to find a place to ride out the weather. Fuck. Where could they possibly go?

CHAPTER TWENTY-NINE

Chelsea ran for her life. If the rain caught her, there would be no evidence of her existence left for anyone to find. The incline made the unstable ground she moved across even more shaky. She wouldn't be surprised if she twisted her ankle or hit a weak spot and slid down over a cliff.

Her back tingled as if someone was watching her. She didn't see anyone, not that she was looking that hard. Her focus needed to stay on getting away. The wind in her ears blocked out any noise that might be around—the screams of dying animals, the cracking of rocks, the start of a rock slide. Damn, she hadn't thought about that. Was that possible?

Then a sound she recognized deep in her soul stopped her. She looked back to see an astounding white dragon with shimmering scales. Her mate, Zaos.

He landed and she wasted no time vaulting onto his nose and over his head to get to his back where, as before, his plates covered her body, strapping her in. They took off immediately. She rested her head on him, her heart rate and breathing near normal. Her magic had to be the reason for that. Her mind went into a complete tailspin.

Beneath her, she felt his muscles roll as his wings pumped them higher. She hoped he knew where he was going. When she felt him angle and sweep around, she looked up. In the wall of rock in front of them was a dark spot that grew bigger the closer they came. Could that be a cave?

She squinted as the wind made her eyes tear up. Yes, Zaos had found a cave for them to hide in. The problem was it was in the center of a shear rock face. No way to climb to it, and the opening wasn't that big. Certainly not for a dragon with wings. How were they going to get inside?

Zaos banked and flew alongside the wall toward the cave. Chelsea felt the scales holding her in place loosen. Her hands tried to grip something, but her body was sliding backward. She screamed, wondering if Zaos had lost his mind. He was letting her fall to her death.

She continued down his back, onto his tail, then she hit the ground hard inside a dark place. A groan escaped her as she sat up, rubbing her head. She was inside the cave. The dingleberry dropped her inside like a bobsled racer rounding the final corner in the Olympics. Shit, she never wanted to try that sport now.

Crawling to the entrance, she looked out to see where Zaos was and how he planned to get inside. The rain wasn't too far away, but it was approaching fast.

The dragon circled several times, probably trying to figure a way into the shelter. With every rotation, Chelsea's pulse increased, her mind becoming more unhinged with the storm closing in and the man she loved still out there.

Finally, she screamed, "Just get your ass over here!" He followed her directions, gliding straight for her. She swallowed hard. *Now what, dumbass?*

she said to herself. *You called him, now haul him in.* Like she had a frigging clue.

The dragon kept coming directly at her. Was he planning on diving through the opening? Holy shit, the diameter was too narrow for his large body. He'd smoosh her into the rock. She climbed to her feet, staying partially bent to not hit her head on the ceiling, and hurried farther into the tunnel.

When she looked behind her, she saw Zaos extend his wings in a back flap, and his feet swung down so his stomach slammed against the rock. The ground shook with the impact.

She ran back and stuck her head over the edge. "Zaos!" He clung to the wall, his fingers impossibly holding onto the rock a few feet under the cave. "Get up here. Hurry up!"

The rain was closer than she wished. Fear tore through her. She and Zaos had gone through enough shit in the past day and a half to die now. "Move it, dragon boy," she ordered.

Zaos hands moved closer, inch by inch, which wasn't fast enough to beat the rain. The pop and sizzle of stone was close enough to hear.

Needing him to climb faster, she lay on her

front side on the cave floor and reached down to slap a hand onto his ass. Grabbing a handful, she squeezed and lifted with all she had. He slid inside as a few drops landed on her arms.

She sucked in a loud breath and gritted her teeth against the pain. More concerned about her man, she scooted back to his head and helped him roll over. "How do you feel?" she asked, knowing it was the stupidest question she could possibly ask.

"I'll survive," he said, letting out a breath. Scratches down his chest dripped blood. A couple of the scrapes were deep enough for her to worry. She took her shirt off and applied pressure to both. The last thing she needed was for him to bleed to death.

She smiled down at him. "I give you a 7.3, and that's only because you stuck the landing. If belly flopping into a wall becomes a sport, you need to practice."

He chuckled then moaned, holding on to his ribs. "Don't make me laugh yet, woman. Give me a minute to heal." He lifted a hand to her face and laid it aside her cheek.

His eyes locked onto hers as he whispered, "I

thought I wouldn't find you in time. I would never forgive myself if I lost you."

She frowned. "This wouldn't have been your fault. You told me to stay in the cave, but I wanted to help. Foolishly, I assumed storms here moved as slowly as those on Earth. Won't do that again."

She lifted her hands to check on the bleeding. To her surprise, the scratches were gone and the gashes were nearly closed. "Damn, you heal fast."

"Yeah," he said, "perk of being a healer, I guess."

"I forgot about that." She put the largest wound on her arm above his mouth. "Give me some breath, baby." He smirked and warm air covered her injury. Instantly the pain went away. He sat up and slid his hands over her bare shoulders and other arm, sending chills through her.

"Are you hurt anywhere else?" he asked, pulling her leg from underneath her. She pointed to another spot on her arm, farther up. He leaned closer and huffed over it.

Hmm, this could get interesting since he was already very naked and within easy reach. Chelsea glanced toward the opening to see the rain staying out of the cave. There shouldn't have been anything else to worry about.

She pointed to her shoulder where there wasn't anything injured, but he breathed over it anyway. Then she placed her finger on the side of her neck. She caught his smile before his lips sucked on her flesh, sending searing heat to her core.

CHAPTER THIRTY

God. She might not make it out of there alive. Every kiss he gave her melted her from the inside and soon she found herself in his arms, her back on something warm and soft and his body pressed over hers. She opened her eyes as he kissed her neck. Glancing to the side, she realized what he'd done. He'd conjured a thick blanket.

"Keep licking me. I'm so hot. I need you," she said, her voice low, desire firing her blood.

Before she knew her, her clothes were gone. This magic business gave him an edge. The breeze made her hot skin break out in goosebumps. Her breath hitched as she watched him kiss his way down her belly. Zaos's head dropped between her legs. It was the most amazing thing she'd felt in her life. His tongue danced over her clit, down to her entrance and even lower to her ass. Then he did it again. She gripped the blanket and moaned.

Need balled in her belly. She gasped at the quick tightening of her muscles. The orgasm caught her completely by surprise. His licks and sucks turned faster. He knew exactly where to touch her. Her muscles tensed and her legs began to shake.

Tension snapped inside her. She pressed her head back against the blanket, her breaths coming out in short pants and let her body lose control. A scream fell from her lips. The burning call for him rushed up her throat and left her mouth at the same time a wave of bliss took her over the edge.

She'd never, not even when she'd played with herself, come as hard as she had that moment. Her legs shook and she slowly uncurled her fingers from the blanket, as she let out a soft moan.

Zaos lifted his head from between her legs. A sexy smile flirted over his lips. "You taste so amazing, love. Like the ripest fruit."

She couldn't understand what came over her,

but hearing him say that to her made her feel amazing. Powerful. Desperate. She wanted- no - she needed him now. One minute he was on his knees in front of her and the next she pushed him onto his back on the blanket. His naked body was a beautiful work of art and she really wanted to get her mouth on him.

"I really like seeing you like this. Naked," she grinned, spreading her hands over his smooth muscled skin. That's what she wanted to touch. Skin. His warm skin and feel that much closer to him.

"You can see me naked whenever you want, love. I'm yours."

Her thoughts exactly.

She ran her nails down his abs, watched him inhale sharply and stopped. Their gazes met and a world of communication happened. They wanted each other, yes, but there was more to it than that. The emotional connection between them was unlike any she'd ever had with another man. She couldn't believe she'd finally found her one. Her man.

She took a long sweep down his body and fell in lust all over again. From his powerful arms down to his rock hard cock, she was more than a little impressed. She was ready for a taste.

Leaning down, she sniffed his neck and moaned. Fucking hell. Even his scent was divine. Like something out of her wet dreams. He smelled of wild animal and hot sex waiting to happen.

He caressed his hands up to her chest, taking her breasts into his hands and fondling her nipples. The man knew just how to touch her.

"God, Zaos. You make me so wet," she moaned, rubbing her nose on the curve of his neck. She licked his hot skin. She loved tasting him. It was weird, but it felt absolutely perfect to do that.

"You sure that wasn't the rain?" he joked.

She laughed and shook her head. "All you."

She took a small lick of his skin and felt her pussy squeeze. Jesus, she was in trouble now. In fact, she couldn't stop herself from licking her way down to his cock. His abs contracted as she slid past them.

He was so hard and hot. And he tasted like red velvet. She licked from root to tip and sighed.

"Sweet Chelsea, do that again," he groaned. "Suck me into your hot lips. I want to watch you slide me down your throat and let my cock out covered in your spit."

She did just that. She twirled her tongue around his cock in circles, using her saliva and his pre-cum to lubricate his length before opening wide and sucking him into her mouth.

"Fuck!" He groaned, pulling her head to his cock. "Your mouth is heaven."

She got lost in her thoughts. There was no turning back now. She sucked him to the back of her throat and used her tongue to flick over his balls.

Before she got more sucks in, he pulled her off him. She was on her knees, in the worship position with her ass in the air and her upper body flat on the blanket. He stood at her back, silent for a moment.

"You are absolutely beautiful," he groaned the words as he squeezed her ass cheeks. The head of his cock pressed up against her wet sheath. "I can't wait to be inside you. Balls deep. Feeling your pussy grip me."

She gasped at the intimate touch of his cock pushing into her. His invasion of her body felt so amazing she could do nothing but grip the blanket and feel. His touch, his smooth glide, everything was perfect. This was the man for her.

He took his time pushing in at first, slowly. Then, once he had pushed and pulled a few times, he took her by surprise and pressed up into her all the way. Breaths rushed out of her lungs in a race out of her body.

"Your body was made for me," he grunted.

Her body throbbed from sucking him hard. A breath later he propelled back and thrust in. And again. His deep strokes didn't stop or slow. They increased with speed and strength. Every thrust felt like she was being branded with a hot iron from the inside.

"*Yesss!*"

Zaos groaned. "I love hearing how much you like me inside you."

She bit her lip and moaned. A fierce need to be wholly his filled her. She needed him to take her. She wanted to be his. All that mattered was what their bodies wanted. Each other.

"You're mine, Chelsea," he grunted with another deep stroke. "I'm branding you. All mine. Is that what you want, love?"

"Yes," she gasped. "I want that," she moaned, the tension rising to a crescendo in her body.

He slid a hand around her front and between her legs to fondle her clit. "Our future is one, now. Just you and me."

That was hard to think about when all her body wanted was for her to come. All she could visualize was the explosion of pleasure when she finally did. But the way he took her body and owned her showed her how much she truly wanted him. Forever.

Chelsea had always followed her instinct and it was screaming at her to take Zaos and never let him go.

"Yes. I'm yours."

He sucked her earlobe into his mouth and bit down lightly. Goosebumps broke across her hot flesh.

He pressed at her clit hard, pinching her and her body convulsed with the force of her orgasm. She curved her back into his body, plastering them together. He continued driving into her in quick plunges. Then she felt the sting and burning on her hip. The pain from the sting and his punishing drives sent her soaring all over again.

He groaned loud, his body vibrating over hers as he came, filling her with his seed.

"You're mine. All mine."

She choked out a breath and glanced at her burning hip. He moved his hand and there, in deep gold lines, a dragon tattoo had appeared. He was right.

"I'm yours."

CHAPTER THIRTY-ONE

As the rain continued outside the cave, Chelsea lay in the arms of the man she'd spend forever with, even if he was an elf/dragon in a different dimension. "I don't get it," she said. "Why does this toxic rain only come here and not the rest of the planet?"

Her mate lay beside her, his head propped up on his hand and bent elbow. "We think it's because of the dead land. The clouds originate over that area, and we never had acid rain until after the ground was poisoned."

That would make sense. On Earth, the ground water evaporated and went into the atmosphere to fuel the clouds and rain. "That piece of land really is a pain in the ass, huh?"

"You mean this ass?" He slid his hand over her hip and under her butt cheek and squeezed. She squealed and laughed as she wiggled to get his hand off.

She pushed against his chest. "Now I've got two pains in the ass."

His brows went up. "You know, I can take care of those pains with a little hot air." He flipped her onto her stomach, leaned over and gently bit her other ass cheek. She laughed and kicked her legs.

"Careful, down there," she called in a singsong voice. "Never know what smell might come out of the cave."

He straddled her hips and kissed his way up her back, then plopped down on his side again. He brushed a strand of hair back. "You are so beautiful. You know that, right?"

Chelsea felt her face blush. She'd always been average looking with bouts of acne in her teen years. Only when she reached her early twenties was she more confident with herself.

"Thank you," she said. "I know you weren't fishing for a compliment, but you're the hottest damn thing I've ever touched." And seen for that matter.

She stared into his stunning eyes, her heart

filled with joy. "I think I'm going to give you a pet name." Zaos's expression wasn't happy. "Elgon."

"Elgon," he sneered, "what kind of pet name is that?"

"You're an elf and a dragon. El gon. Elgon." She liked the idea.

He grinned and leaned down to kiss her. Did that mean he loved it or hated it? When he pulled back, she noted how quiet it had gotten. "Hey," she said, "the rain has stopped." She shimmied to the front of the cave and looked out. "Oh my god!" Her breath was swept away. The green valley below was gone, replaced by mud, except for the fire lilies that miraculously survived.

The forests that were so full of foliage and life were black sticks jabbing up from rocky ground. Again, photos of a wooded area of California after a massive wildfire could belong to what she looked at now. Had a nuclear bomb dropped?

"This is what happens every time it rains?" She just couldn't believe it.

"Yes," he answered. "You see why we abandoned living in the trees and went into the caves."

She could only nod. Chelsea stared into the valley of mud, speechless. Then she noticed green patches growing around all the fire lilies. The patches overlapped each other and spread out in all directions. The grass was coming back.

When the grassy section below them hit the base of the mountain, it stopped. But in other directions, it kept going.

The tall black shells of trees fell away as a new trunks with fresh bark stood in their place. Leaves sprouted on quickly forming branches. The forests came alive in the same linear pattern they had died.

Once again, she was flabbergasted.

"Wow," Zaos said. "Hadn't seen that before. I wondered how everything was back to normal within a few hours."

She looked at him, disbelieving his comment. "Are you serious? You never saw any of this happen?"

"No," he said, shaking his head. "I was smart enough to stay inside the caves until the ground dried. Otherwise your feet would melt off."

All right, she'd give him that. She looked out again and almost the entire valley was green once more. It was totally wicked how the grass came back in circles around each lily and spread until it reached another growing area.

But if the ground was still toxic until it dried,

how had the grass grown? Then the image of the little girl who was poisoned by a plant soon after they arrived yesterday flashed in her mind.

"Oh my god!" She smacked her forehead with her palm. "Why hadn't I thought of that before."

She must've startled Zaos seeing how somber his face was. "Thought of what?" he asked.

"The dead land is *poisoned*," she said.

"Yes, love. I'm glad you understand that. After I've said it ten times already."

She smacked his shoulder. "Stop being a smart ass. This is serious." She knocked her head with her palm again.

"I can tell," he said. "Would you like to whack me in the head next?" He wiggled his hips, making his cock awaken. His naughty smile and twinkle in his eye almost made her forget what she was thinking.

She huffed then put her clothes on. "Fly me to the caves so I can talk with Gorwin."

"What do you want me to do?" he asked as if he were about to disagree with her.

"You need to go to your king father and have him meet me and Gorwin where the training field meets the dead land."

"Why?" he asked.

She just grinned. "Wait and see."

After a bit of trial and error getting her out of the cave without plunging to her death, Chelsea stood in front of King Gorwin as he prepared midday meal. If her plan worked, he wouldn't have to be doing this much longer.

She stalled a bit too long and the king retired to his private rooms. Kicking herself, she tentatively approached the door with a guard standing beside it.

"Hi," she said with a smile. "I need to speak with the king—"

"He is not available," the guy shot at her.

"But this is rather important. You see—"

"The king is not available," he nearly shouted, drawing attention from those in the food line. Dammit. This was not going as planned. Hopefully, Zaos and his king father would wait.

She heard a *click* and the doors to the royal's sanctuary opened. "I grant her permission to enter."

The guard scowled at her then held the door open. Chelsea hurried in before he tried to hit her backside with it. What she saw made her swallow hard. The living space was an eclectic mix of masculinity and feminine softness. One side had large furniture that was well worn.

The other side had dainty chairs upholstered in a creamy material. A tea service sat on a tray on a round ottoman between the four seats. What looked to be a form of piano stood behind the seating arrangement. The biggest difference between the two sides was that one looked brand new, unused, while the other was the opposite.

She'd never seen the queen, his mate, in the day and a half she'd been here. And why didn't she use the cute settee? In fact, the whole side of the room appeared not lived in. Did the king not have a mate?

Not having a female to temper his aggression and needs, she now understood why he was such a grump, yet—dare she say—caring? He wouldn't let her go to the dragons by herself. He only complied after Zaos agreed to go. The king wanted to keep her safe even though it seemed he was just being a dick.

The king cleared his throat, drawing her attention. "You have information from the drag-ons?" he asked. He looked her up and down. "I guess they provided a place of safety from the storm and did not eat you."

"No, sir. They didn't eat me. But a lot happened in a short amount of time."

"Continue," he said.

"Yes, of course," she replied, "but could you come with me to the training field first? There's something we need to discuss there."

"I do not like surprises, little girl. Tell me of what you mean."

Yeah, of course, he would be grumpy. "Zaos and I have spoken with the dragon king and I want us to negotiate there. Zaos has gone to get the—"

A thunderous noise erupted outside the door. A loud shout sent her blood running cold. "The dragons are attacking."

CHAPTER THIRTY-TWO

After dressing and kissing his mate, Zaos headed uphill toward the dragon's territory once again. Stepping through the magical divide, he was greeted by the same two dragons, except this time they bowed to him.

Great, he thought. *No keeping this secret very secret.*

One of the dragons roared with a return roar on its heels. That must be how they communicated in dragon form. Zaos gestured toward the stairs. "Can I go up?" The dragon nodded.

This time, the view of the levels was much different than before. People were pulling things out of notches in the walls and from the ground where they had buried them. Oh, they were protecting their stuff by putting it in the ground.

Living in the caves, his people never had to deal with such problems. Yet, he bet the dragons never had to worry about the ceiling crushing them into the floor.

His father met him on the steps. "You're safe," the king said. "I was so worried. To have known you for such a short time and then never see you again."

"My mate and I found a cave to take shelter in."

"Good," the king turned, "come up with me. Stay a while."

"Father—" he said. The man in front of him spun around, tears welling. Zaos wondered what made the man this emotional suddenly.

The king place PLACED a hand on each of Zaos's shoulders. "You do not know how I've longed to hear my son call me—" His head lowered and he cleared his throat. Zaos didn't know what to say. He'd spent his whole life hating the father he never met. He had a lot of making up to do. First things first.

"Father," he said again and the king smiled at him, "I need you to come with me to the elves' training field. My mate has had an epiphany and wants to surprise you, me, and King Gorwin next to the dead land."

"The dead land?" he said. "Yes, I will come, but I need to have my security with me." Zaos agreed and waited in the cottage he and his mate had visited earlier. Several moments later, the king returned. "I am ready to go with you."

He headed for the door, but his father stopped him. "It is a far walk to where we need to go. Let me move us with my power."

His father placed a hand on his shoulder again, and in the blink of an eye, Zaos stood on the mountainside just above the stretch of forest that bordered one side of the field. The swath of green cutting through the forest was vacant. Usually at this time, his men were eating midday meal.

The sun was hot, standing on the barren rocks. "Father, you and your men can wait in the trees where it's cooler. I need to find my mate." He turned to see how many the king had with him.

"Oh, dwarf shit," his head dropped into his lifted hand. "Father, I thought you were bringing only your security. Not the entire dragon army." He noted many females within the group.

His dad glanced back. "This *is* my security. They are in elven form, not dragon."

Zaos wiped his hand down his face. "All right, have everyone wait in the forest next to the field. I'll return."

Zaos jogged toward the cave entrance to check what was keeping his mate. He thought she would've been there already. He heard the loud thump of many feet hitting the ground. Then he saw who made those stomps.

"Halt!" he shouted. The men dressed in battle gear came to an abrupt stop.

"The dragons are attacking," a few of the elves hollered.

Double dwarf shit. "No, they are here in peace. I brought them to negotiate a resolution to our long war against them."

"How do we know they won't attack?" came from the growing group.

He sighed. "Because they have many females among them." If anything would keep the men from fighting, knowing they could injure a female would hold their arrows.

The elves mumbled among themselves.

"Zaos," he heard his mate's voice in back of the group. The elves stepped aside, creating a path to his mate and the king. They hurried toward him. Chelsea hugged him then leaned back to look up at him. "They think the dragons are here to fight. You have to stop them."

King Gorwin growled. "I don't trust them. How do we know they aren't hiding, waiting for us to expose ourselves?"

Zaos opened his mouth, then closed it. The king had a point. He told the dragons to wait in the forest, which absolutely seemed like they were hiding for attack.

Zaos raised a hand for quiet. "My King, I advised the dragon king to wait with his males *and females* in the cooler shade of the forest on the far side of the training field." Gorwin raised a brow on the word *females*.

The king nodded. "We will remain on this side of the field in the trees, opposite of the enemy."

Chelsea slammed fists onto her hips. "They are no longer the enemy. They have no idea about the cave-ins or anything. Has anyone ever talked to the dragons?" The king scowled at her. She leaned forward, her face scrunched back at him. Demon's hell, his mate finally stepped over the line.

Zaos pulled her behind him and bowed his

head. "My King, the dragon leader is ready to discuss with you."

"Let's get this over with," Gorwin said, striding through the forest.

Zaos followed, his mate in tow. He leaned over to her. "You know what you're doing, right?"

She grinned at him. "Of course. Oh, wait. I need a fire lily." She stepped to the side and held out her hand. "Dagger, please." He watched as she cut the ground around the flower, lifted it, then shook off the dirt around the roots. "Okay, let's go." They jogged to catch up with the king. Zaos gave her a quick kiss then rushed ahead to get the dragon king.

Racing across the strip of grass that split the woods, he didn't see any of the dragons. Were they hiding? Had they left? He stepped past the first trees and his father greeted him.

The dragon king informed him, "My people are keeping their presence minimal to not give the impression of an invasion."

"Thank you, Father. You are smarter than I."

"No, son. I understand your people's frustration and their want for revenge. I don't want any of my people changing over to protect me and end up killing the whole dark elf species."

"I appreciate that, too."

Zaos watched for his mate to emerge. When she did, he guided his father and king of the dragons to the edge where life met death.

CHAPTER THIRTY-THREE

Chelsea could throw-up at this point. She had no idea if her thought process was free of errors. But it all made sense. Add to her uncertainty the fact that both sides had a ton of people who could die if one thing went wrong, she was just peachy.

With the king at her side, she stepped onto the grass from the trees. When nothing happened, no flying arrows, no giant dragons flattening elves, she continued to the edge of the field and stood where Zaos met her. His gorgeous smile eased the butterflies in her stomach.

The elven king tilted his head forward. "Hello, Larongar. It's been a long time."

Her jaw dropped at the social niceties the elf

displayed. But in reality, the grumpy old guy wasn't so bad. Just seemed like it.

"Nindro." The dragon king also tilted his head toward the other king. "It has been a long time. Perhaps too long."

These two knew each other on a first-name basis? They had to be shitting her. She didn't— Zaos nudged her with his elbow.

"Uh, yeah. Thank you both for coming," she said like an idiot. She could've kicked herself for being so unprepared for this. That wasn't like her. She usually did her homework to understand both sides before the soon-to-be-divorced couple arrived. At least she knew each side's situation.

She nodded at Gorwin. "For years, your clan has been forced underground to escape the storms, live under the threat of collapsing cave walls, the possibility of having no females or children to grow the group, your magic slowly dying from loss of connection with nature, and..."

Geesh, wasn't that enough shit for one people to deal with? But there was another she'd thought of—Zaos leaned over and whispered *mates*.

"Ah, right, the lack of opportunity for mates because you refuse to allow other species to marry into the dark elves." At least the king had the decency to cringe at how bad that sounded.

She turned to her mate's father and smiled. "Leader Larongar, for years, your community has been blessed with continuing generations so much so that some of you are in danger from having to live in far outlying areas. Like the dark elves, you are forced underground when the storms come. And you'd probably prefer to have one level instead of several." She was guessing, but she would if she were him. He gave her a nod.

"Good news," she said, "if this works like I think it will, then almost all of your problems will be solved."

The two kings shared a look of surprise.

Chelsea knelt on the grass, ready to plunges the knife into the dirt when mass confusion erupted. Zaos grabbed her around the waist, yanking her away from the dirt. When he set her down, she understood what was happening.

In the clearing itself, between the dragons and dark elves, stood her sister and Tylen and half the village ready to fight.

"Avery!" she hollered and ran to her sister, giving her a huge hug. "What are you doing here?" Chelsea asked.

Avery snorted. "Like I'm seriously going to leave my sister stranded with dark elves."

"Aww," Chelsea said, "I love you, too, sis. But I'm not stranded."

Avery harrumphed. "Then why are dark elves hiding over there and dragons on that side? They look ready to battle, leaving you unsecure."

Zaos stood beside her, frown on his face. Chelsea wrapped her arm around his and pulled him closer. "Since we are in real life and not a magical abyss, I'll introduce my guy again. Avery, this is my mate, Zaos...shit, I don't even know your last name."

He kissed the top of her head. "With a small clan, we don't need surnames. All know who Zaos is."

She grinned at him. "I bet they do." She was surprised when her mate's cheeks flushed. He was so adorable.

"So what's going on?" Avery asked.

"Right, I'm hoping something works that will keep these two from war from now on."

Avery turned to Tylen. "It's okay, love. You can let them go now." Suddenly, dark elves and dragons ran toward the group in the middle. Then they froze mid-step.

Avery turned to her. "Chel, you need to tell the folks to chill out. Tylen will only release his magic if he knows his people are safe."

Good god. Leave it to her sister to complicate things. She turned to the kings. "Guys, will you tell your respective people to stay back? The light elves are here to visit me."

"With weapons drawn?" Gorwin grunted.

Chelsea pressed her lips into a thin line. "Just tell them. Please," she begged. "I really want to soak in a hot tub right now and there are none here, as far as I know."

Both rulers made announcements to back off. Chelsea took for granted even though the people were frozen with Tylen's magic, they could still hear. When released, those who ran forward retreated.

Chelsea turned back to the dead land and where she had been kneeling. She was tired and wanted this to work. Otherwise, she'd be eternally shamed in this whole dimension after causing such a ruckus with three species.

On her knees again, Chelsea stabbed the knife into the dirt to make a small hole a few inches deep. When the knife tip began to melt, she freaked out a little. Quickly, she set the fire lily in the hole and shoveled dirt around it.

Standing back, they all stared at the red and orange tendrils floating on the air.

"Well," Gorwin said, "at least it's still alive." He picked a blade of grass and dropped it on the rough land. Instantly, it poofed into a flame and was gone.

Behind her came a sweet little voice. "It's a fire lily. Where's the fire?" Ryo asked the same question she had when the girl in the village was poisoned. Zaos picked up the boy and stepped back from the edge.

"Well," she said, looking to the dragon king since her mate held the boy, "Larongar, will you do the honors?"

The dragon king stepped forward and in human form sent a stream of fire onto the plant. When he stopped. The flower was black and crumbled into ash.

Avery laughed. "Looks like another one bites the dust."

Chelsea could not believe her sister said that. Fortunately, no one knew what she was quoting.

"Or," Avery continued, "all we are is dust in the wind."

"Avery," Chelsea scolded, but couldn't keep the smile off her face. "Those were really good. I never would've thought of them."

She let out a sigh. Shit, shit, shit. It didn't work.

Larongar whispered to her, "What did you expect to happen?"

"I had hoped the fire lily would heal the ground like it did after the storm. All the grass came back around the lilies first. The flower healed the toxic poison."

"This is really bad stuff, love," Zaos said. "Maybe you need more than one lily."

Ryo wriggled out of Zaos's arms. "I'll get one, okay?" The child searched the field and found one nearby that wasn't trampled by guests. He plucked it from the ground and ran to her. Chelsea held her hand out for him to give it to her. But instead, in true childlike fashion, he bypassed her and headed straight for the dirt.

"I can do it, okay," he said. Zaos reached out and snagged the little one's shirt just before his foot landed in the dirt. The lily in his hand fell onto the dry land. "Now, put fire on it, okay," Ryo said, patting Zaos's thigh with his hand.

Zaos gave her a strange expression then turned to the boy. "Okay," he repeated.

"That's a great idea," she said. "At least you won't fry the poor thing."

"But don't you want to plant it?" he asked.

Chelsea shrugged. "Might as well try this. There's no roots on it anyway. I'll dig up another one."

Zaos handed the child to his birth father for safe keeping then moved closer to the dead land. Two things then dawned on her. One, past healers said it would take a combination of things to heal the land. And two, Zaos had the Breath of Life. A double whammy of healing sources. In her heart, she knew this was the answer.

The fire from her mate didn't burn the lily, but it didn't seem to help any either. Before their eyes, the flower soaked into the ground. Sucked down like a toy ship in a whirlpool.

In its place, the dirt turned dark in color, then like a race car at the starting line, it spread in all directions. Chelsea jumped and clasped her hands together.

Larongar kneeled and hesitantly jabbed his fingers into the ground. He stood with a handful and sniffed it. He smiled and let the dark dirt fall from his hand.

"It's soil," he said loudly. "It's fertile, healthy soil."

Gasps rang through the crowd. Chelsea sighed with relief. She hadn't had the recipe completely right, but close enough.

Someone clapped their hands and stepped from the trees. Chelsea looked over her shoulder to see Tel with a snotty sneer. "Excellent," he said, but Chelsea really didn't believe he meant it. "We can now plant seeds, but we are still confined to the caves. It will take eons for the land to grow into a forest that can hold us. You haven't really solved any of our problems, girl."

Chelsea shifted her weight to one foot. "What is your problem, Tel? Do you just enjoy being the asshole of the group?"

He shrugged a shoulder. "Only pointing out the obvious. The battle for living on the mountain continues."

Shit, he was right. They needed a way to make the land sprout quickly and grow fast. Sounded like a job for magic. Not just regular magic, but royal magic.

"King Gorwin," she said, "how about making the dirt grow plants like you do for the meals."

The king's eyes widened. "I am no longer strong enough to do even a fraction of this." His arm swept toward the newly cleansed, newly healed ground. He bowed, stepping back. "I cannot be of any help."

Tel laughed.

CHAPTER THIRTY-FOUR

Hope coursed through Zaos's heart when he realized his mate's plan. She was a genius and gorgeous. Then, just as quickly, the hope died. His king was right. He didn't have magic powerful enough to do much.

Again, without a mate, Zaos feared Gorwin would soon die by his own choice. He'd been alive for thousands of years and had no reason to go on. He would be expected to take over. At least some of their problems had been solved.

"I can help with that," Chelsea's sister said, stepping forward. "I am a naturea parrera." The kings looked at each other, confusion as their expression.

"Love," Tylen whispered to Avery, "it's natura patera."

She waved off the correction. "Whatever."

Zaos's mouth dropped open. "A natura patera is unheard of. It belongs to the legends of the elves."

"I know," Avery said. "Isn't that cool? King Gorwin, go ahead and do your thing. I'll help after you get started."

Gorwin looked at Zaos. "Do my thing?"

Zaos shook his head. "She means do your magic." He motioned toward the dead land. The king went to a knee and dipped his fingers into the soil. A moment later, a green stem popped up on the border of the two land types. Avery laid her hand on his shoulder and closed her eyes.

Gorwin's body stiffened with Avery's touch. Green continued to spurt up around the older man's hand. "More," the king said. He fell onto both knees and dug in up to his wrists. New plants matured into full growth around his touch while farther out new sprouts emerged.

"More!" he hollered."

Avery tightened her hold on his shoulder, her eyes squeezed closed.

In the distance, shoots and finger-thin trees

burst out of the dirt. Farther and farther, the king's magic spread.

"More!"

Avery put her other hand on his other shoulder. Magic poured into the land. Zaos couldn't see any farther, but he knew the land continued to come alive with nature. The thin tree grew wider and wider, like blowing up a balloon. Other saplings sprang up, growing thicker as they watched.

"More," Gorwin mumbled. His arms and legs trembled, his head hung down. Zaos wasn't sure how much more the old elf could take.

A full grown forest stood before them, the trees becoming thicker and thicker the longer the magic poured through the land.

A female light elf elbowed him to the side and yanked Avery away from the king. "Enough," the female said, "you'll hurt him." Gorwin slumped into the woman's arms. She held him close, rocking, and combing back his hair with her fingers.

Chelsea went to her sister and held onto her as they stared at the couple. "Holy shit," Avery said. "Are they mates?" her sister called over her shoulder. "Tylen, come here, babe."

Avery asked the elf king, "Is Velatha his mate or is she just being nice to him?"

Tylen breathed deeply. "I'd say they are mates."

"Holy shit," both girls said together.

Tylen turned to face the crowd. "Maybe, but it seems normal at the moment."

Zaos whipped his head around to see a huge mass of dragons, light elves, and dark elves mingling. Many were paired off. Mates?

He glanced at his king, the old face beaming, looker younger than he had in eons. Zaos merged into the group, seeking out his men. Darfin held a female dragon's hands and stared into her eyes. Another man had the same look with a light elf.

His only worry now was whether or not the king would allow mixed marriages. Since his own mate was a light elf, Zaos believed the king's mind had been opened to the richness of diversity.

Zaos looked around for his mate. She was no longer with her sister. He made his way toward Avery who leaned against her mate.

"Avery," Zaos asked, "where is Chelsea?"

His mate's sister scanned the area. "She was here a little bit ago."

Damnation, this was twice in one sun cycle

that he'd lost his other half. They needed to mate soon so he could keep track of her through their link. He had a feeling that would come into use several times throughout their time together.

He called out her name, hoping she'd come to him. After several attempts and no reply, he became frantic. Where could she have gone? He saw Ryo crying with dirt on his face and arm. Zaos rushed to the little one.

On a knee, he rubbed his thumb on the angelic cheeks. "Why are you crying?"

Zaos held up the boy's fragile arm with scratches and blew on it.

"Tel," Ryo cried. "He pushed me down and took Chelsea away." Zaos barely hung on to control of his dragon. He'd never experienced his animal being so aggressive. But they hadn't ever been missing a mate, either.

Ryo sniffled. "She had to go with him or he'd hurt me."

"Which way did they go?" he asked the boy. His little finger pointed toward the mountain. Dwarf shit, that wasn't much help. "Go find one of the females and stay with her for a while."

Ryo nodded and ran toward a group of children gathered around one such female.

Zaos hurried through the gathering in the direction the boy indicated. The waterfall was in this general direction. Would Tel take her there? Did he even know about it?

Needing to get there fast, he let his dragon come forward, drawing the attention of many. He didn't care. Everyone might as well know who he really was.

He climbed the air with each downstroke of his wings. Quickly, he reached the upper most ridge and set down. From here, he could see long distances. Taking in the dead land, he saw no poisoned dirt. The full area had been returned to them.

Turning to the other direction, he saw what he feared. Tel was at the oasis. But he didn't see Chelsea standing anywhere. Zaos then took notice of what Tel was kicking on the grass. If not for his mate's different clothing, he wouldn't have thought she was being beaten. He dove toward them, flying as fast as he could.

Tel bashed his shoes into his mate's sides time and again. When the bastard kicked her head, the dragon roared. Tel looked up and smiled.

Draped over his shoulder, Tel set an arrow in his bow and sent it at him. Zaos's dragon raised his head, exposing his underside. The arrow slammed into a scale and skidded off. Was that because his covering was so slippery?

Another arrow targeted him. It hit his shoulder and slid across his back harmlessly. The bastard elf shot off several in a row, all useless against his body armor.

Zaos was almost to them. He would grind Tel into the ground, rip him apart. His sharp eyes saw the elf grin and kick his mate hard enough to roll her to the water's edge. With an especially hard kick from him, she dropped into the water. Tel, standing there, grinned at him.

His mind switched off, animal survival instincts taking control. *Mate. Save our mate.* In a nosedive, he tucked his wings into his sides, eyes locked on the water where their mate went in. A hairsbreadth from the water, he threw his wings into a back flap then shifted to his elf form, plunging into the water.

Her body wasn't at the place she went in. He let the current take him to the pile of rocks where the water disappeared into the ground. He saw her, body half on small boulders.

His heart ached so badly, he nearly doubled

over. She wasn't dead. Couldn't be. He'd had her only one day. One fucking day.

When he reached her, he lifted her out of the water onto the rocks where her upper body rested. Blood caked her face around her nose and mouth. Bruises shadowed her cheek and arm. He could only imagine how her ribs looked.

He kissed her cheek, blowing on it lightly. The bruise lightened. If only he could climb inside her and spread his Breath of Life on her internal injuries. He smelled the blood seeping into her body from deep wounds.

"Chelsea," he whispered, not strong enough to talk any louder. "Chelsea, wake up, baby. You're not leaving yet. You have more challenges to solve." No response, but her chest moved slightly.

He couldn't stop the flow of tears that tore from his eyes. His emotions were too wild, too robust to hold inside. He fought hard, worked hard, and loved hard. He'd attribute those traits to his birth father.

He rested his forehead gently on hers, holding her shoulders in his lap. He decided right then that he'd let Tel kill him so he could join his mate in the hereafter.

"Hey," his mate breathed out. Her unswollen eyelid lifted enough for her to see him.

He cupped her face in his hand, thumb brushing her cheek. "Hey," he repeated.

She licked her lips. "Tell my sister I love her. I love you, too. Probably since I first hit you on the way out the cave." The corners of her mouth raised. "Kiss me," she demanded.

Feeling this was her way of saying goodbye, he put all his emotion, all his love into the kiss. Her lips parted, letting him taste her, breathe her in, one last time. He pulled back a touch and hovered over her mouth, hearing air rattle in her chest with every inhale.

"I love you, Chelsea. I will see you soon on the other side." Her breath slipped out, none going back in.

A roar filled with anguish and pain ripped from his throat. His mate had died. He felt empty. An endless chasm opened inside him, taking his will to go on without her.

Tel came into view, smile on his face. "Did your mate die? I'm so sorry you didn't get what you want. Actually this turned out better than I'd imagined. Hope you had the chance to fuck her last night. What a waste if not. She was so fuckable. I could hardly wait until three days were up. Well, don't have to worry about that now."

Though he'd vowed to die beside her, the fury that filled his chest wouldn't allow him to go quietly. He would kill Tel, then go on. He laid her body on the rock then gathered his strength and determination to do what his dragon demanded. Blood.

Zaos leaped up, not ready for the arrow Tel loosed. Zaos twisted, but not enough. The shaft entered just below the shoulder, missing his heart by inches.

His dragon came to the surface, but he wouldn't let it take control. He wrapped his fingers around the piece of wood and pulled it out with another roar, snapping it in two before throwing it to the ground.

"Tel," he said, "I've put up with you far longer than any other elf would. I'm going to relieve the king of your vile presence. You will no longer threaten to take females against their will or any other stupid-ass idea that comes to your small brain."

Tel's head tilted. "More strange words—stupid ass. Where did you go to return so different?"

"That's not of your concern, dickhead," Zaos replied. "Time for you to die." Before he could make a move, his enemy shot another arrow. Prepared, Zaos dodged to the side into a somersault, coming up with a fist-size rock in his hand. His arm circled around, launching the missile at his opponent.

His aim wasn't Tel's flesh but the weapon in his hand. The stone smashed into the back of his hand holding the arched wood. So his aim was off a bit. The sound of crunching bones was satisfying.

Tel dropped the bow and cradled his hand against himself. He would heal quickly, so Zaos raced for the weapon, scooping it up while avoiding a kick from the other elf. He crushed the wood between in his hands.

Having only one line of defense, Tel pulled an arrow out of the quiver on his back. He held it out like a dagger, jabbing it at Zaos while he backed away.

There was no place for the elf to go. He was sure only one of them would make it out of here. He stepped forward, forcing Tel toward the end of the stream where the big boulders had piled up. Where his mate's body rested.

Tel rambled on about how he would rule the clan once he killed the pathetic king and took females from other kingdoms. He delighted in the thought of having his own harem. Zaos shook his head, disgusted, saying nothing.

As far back as Tel could go, the dickhead lunged forward, the small spear grazing Zaos's side. Instinctively, Zaos's arms stretched out, shoving away the elf.

Tel stumbled against the boulders, losing his balance. As he steadied himself, a rock the size of his fist came out of the pile and slammed into the side of his head. The bastard reeled, hands on his head. Then an arm snaked out of the rocks, fingers yanking his pant and leg sideways.

Tel slipped on water-covered loose gravel and fell onto the boulder that Chelsea had said looked like someone had scooped out a dollop of ice cream. The indentation was filled with water instead of pebbles like before. But when Tel screamed and smoke rose from him, Zaos made a correction.

It wasn't just water that was in the tub-like space, but acid water from the rain not long ago.

Still screaming, Tel threw himself off the rock. His hands were smoking while his fingers slowly burned into ashes. Since the front of his shirt was soaked, his chest and stomach were being eaten away. He fell to the ground, a squirming lump of flesh with legs.

Apparently, he splashed his face when he landed on the rock. The side of his cheek had dissolved, revealing teeth, gums, and muscle. That wasn't a nice sight. Rather gross, actually.

Giving the decomposing body a wide berth, Zaos made his way to where the hand that pulled on Tel lay.

"Chelsea?" He slid to his knees, lifting her to lean against him. He held her in his arms and rocked side to side. How was she alive? He didn't care too much about the how, as long as she breathed.

She patted his arms. "Hey, mate, you're about to recrush my ribs that just got uncrushed." Immediately, his hold loosened.

He twisted around to see her face. "What are you talking about? How are you alive?"

She grinned. "Kiss me and I'll show you."

He gladly covered her mouth with his. Unexpectedly, the air from his lungs was drawn out of his body. His mate's chest expanded fully...with his air, his breath. The Breath of Life. She laid her head against his arm.

"That's more like it," she sighed. "Now the rest of me can heal."

He couldn't believe she was alive. The brief kiss he gave her before fighting Tel kept her living. He wanted to absorb her into his body so he could be as close as possible. His body tingled down to his soul with his mate alive and beside him.

"You know," she said, "you've used way too many figures of speech and even shook my hand when we met, which no one else has a clue about. And you're the only one who hasn't sniffed me and asked what my other half is."

"Really?" He thought he done a damnation good job of being a normal elf, except to Tel, obviously.

"So," she continued, "when were you on Earth?"

He leaned back and laughed. "You are too smart for you own damnation good, you know that, right?" She smiled. "Let me tell you a story about a witch with a white streak in her black hair that opened a portal to a strange planet because said elf's mate lived there."

Her eyes popped wide and her jaw dropped. "You're shitting me."

"And that, my love, is exactly why she left me there for a century. I wouldn't have understood half the things my human mate would've said without learning her culture. I guess learning how earthlings functioned was important enough to make a difference."

"Nah," Chelsea shook her head. "I would've loved you no matter how silly you spoke."

EPILOGUE

*Z*aos and Chelsea stood at the edge of the training field, looking back at the friends and couples that recently met in this same location. Just about all the dark elf men had found their mates among the others. And talk about a one-eighty flip. She barely recognized them.

And speaking of barely recognizing, the former elf king was a new man with his mate by his side. She'd always thought Velatha was born to be a queen.

In the front, her cousins, Daphne, Wren, and Lilah, and her sister with her mate all smiled too big at her. Something was up. From family gatherings, she knew her cousins better than they thought.

Zaos cleared his throat and everyone quieted. "First off, I'd like to thank everyone for attending this informal event. We have two things to accomplish. I'd like to start with the dedication of our new home.

"We once again are among nature, living in the habitat we were meant to be in. With so many new mates, our village will be a blend of several cultures that will, in time, become the best of each.

"Since King Gorwin has stepped down from his royal position to spend time with his new mate, and Leader Larongar has retired to be with the children more, I am, in both villages, now the residing ruler."

Cheers rose and his name was chanted over and over until he raised his hand for quiet. "So, being the ruler of each, I'm now combining them to make one city where everyone is welcome, no matter where they are from."

More cheers. She was so proud of her mate. He truly cared for other's wellbeing and happiness. He wanted this coming together to work so badly that he'd promised to spend weeks with her planning how to run such a large village without the problem cities on Earth had encountered.

"Now that we all are one group, elves and dragons together, I designate the name of our village Elgon."

"What?" Chelsea hollered, not heard over the crowd's whooping.

He smiled at her. "Sorry, love," he said, "you'll have to find another pet name for me."

Oh, she'd have no problem finding different names for him. She had a whole slew just waiting for the right opportunity to use.

From the crowd came, "What's the second thing we are here for?"

Her cousins squished closer together, giggling and bouncing on their toes. They were such a crazy trio. She wondered if they had mates elsewhere on this planet. They'd have to travel each kingdom to find out. And, boy, she felt sorry for those guys.

When she glanced at Zaos, he was kneeling beside her, holding up a black velvet box with a stunning diamond ring.

"Chelsea, I almost lost you once, well, twice actually in the same day," those nearby chuckled, "but I intend to never have you far from my side.

Chelsea, my love, my life, my soul, would you marry me?"

She couldn't get her answer out quick enough. Yes, she'd marry him.

THAT NIGHT CHELSEA was exhausted from the eventful day. Her cousins wanted to leave a couple hours ago, so she gave them her gemstone for the three needed to open a portal.

So she was quite surprised when her grandmom showed up.

"Chelsea," Grandmom said, "I'm so proud of you and all you've done to make our home a better place. I know the other kings are eager to meet you and Zaos. We can make plans for that later."

"I'm astonished your cousins are still there. I figured they'd want to come back early since they have work tomorrow."

She looked at Zaos, her heart nearly falling into her stomach.

"Uh, Grandmom," she said, "the girls returned a while ago."

She watched her grandmother's eye widen.

"No, they haven't."

"Oh no," she bit her lip.

Grandmom twisted her hands around each other. "Were you there when they left?" Grandmom asked. "As in did you hold one of the stones?"

Chelsea shook her head. "No. I was in the middle of planting carrots, so I gave them mine."

"Oh, darn," the elder said.

"Why does that matter?" She had a feeling she wouldn't like the answer.

"Those particular stones are tuned to my magic and any person who carries my blood magic. That would be you and Avery."

"And what happens when there is no one with your blood magic using the stones?" Chelsea took a deep breath and held it, ready to freak out if the answer was what she thought.

Grandmom stopped pacing on Earth's side. "The portal that opens could be to any dimension, during any time."

Oh no. Where could they be?

The End...of this story and the beginning of a whole new adventure.

Fae King

Elf King

Dark King

Fire King

Read them all and be sure to check out the upcoming

Crystal Kingdom: New Worlds

and if you have some young adults at home and would like for them to read the CLEAN and

SWEET version of the Crystal Kingdom, be sure
to check out

Fae Queen

Elf Queen

Dark Queen

Fire Queen

Get them all!

ABOUT THE AUTHOR

New York Times and USA Today Bestselling Author

Hi! I'm Milly Taiden. I love to write sexy stories featuring fun, sassy heroines with curves and growly alpha males with fur. My books are a great way to satisfy your craving for paranormal romance with action, humor, suspense and happily ever afters.

I live in Florida with my hubby, our kids, and our fur babies: Speedy, Stormy and Teddy. I have a serious addiction to chocolate and cake.

I love to meet new readers, so come sign up for my newsletter and check out my Facebook page. We always have lots of fun stuff going on there.

SIGN UP FOR MILLY'S NEWSLETTER FOR LATEST NEWS!

http://eepurl.com/pt9q1

Find out more about Milly here:
www.millytaiden.com
milly@millytaiden.com

ALSO BY MILLY TAIDEN

Find out more about Milly Taiden here:

Email: millytaiden@gmail.com

Website: http://www.millytaiden.com

Facebook: http://www.facebook.com/millytaidenpage

Twitter: https://www.twitter.com/millytaiden

ALSO BY MILLY TAIDEN

If you liked this story, you might also enjoy the following by Milly Taiden:

The Crystal Kingdom

Fae King *Book One*

Elf King *Book Two*

Dark King *Book Three*

Fire King *Book Four*

Casters & Claws

Spellbound in Salem *Book One*

Seduced in Salem *Book Two*

Spellstruck in Salem *Book Three*

Surrendered in Salem *Book Four*

Alpha Geek

Alpha Geek: *Knox*

Alpha Geek: *Zeke*

Alpha Geek: *Gray*

Alpha Geek: *Brent*

Savage Kiss *Book Two*

Savage Hunger *Book Three*

Savage Caress *Book Four*

Drachen Mates

Bound in Flames *Book One*

Bound in Darkness *Book Two*

Bound in Eternity *Book Three*

Bound in Ashes *Book Four*

Federal Paranormal Unit

Wolf Protector *Federal Paranormal Unit Book One*

Dangerous Protector *Federal Paranormal Unit Book Two*

Unwanted Protector *Federal Paranormal Unit Book Three*

Deadly Protector *Federal Paranormal Unit Book Four*

Paranormal Dating Agency

Twice the Growl *Book One*

Geek Bearing Gifts *Book Two*

The Purrfect Match *Book Three*

Curves 'Em Right *Book Four*

Tall, Dark and Panther *Book Five*

The Alion King *Book Six*

There's Snow Escape *Book Seven*

Scaling Her Dragon *Book Eight*

In the Roar *Book Nine*

Scrooge Me Hard *Short One*

Bearfoot and Pregnant *Book Ten*

All Kitten Aside *Book Eleven*

Oh My Roared *Book Twelve*

Piece of Tail *Book Thirteen*

Kiss My Asteroid *Book Fourteen*

Scrooge Me Again *Short Two*

Born with a Silver Moon *Book Fifteen*

Also, check out the **Paranormal Dating Agency World on Amazon**

Or visit http://mtworldspress.com

ALSO BY MILLY TAIDEN

Raging Falls

Miss Taken *Book One*

Miss Matched *Book Two*

Miss Behaved *Book Three*

Miss Behaved *Book Three*

Miss Mated *Book Four*

Miss Conceived *Book Five (Coming Soon)*

Alphas in Fur

Bears

Fur-Bidden *Book One*

Fur-Gotten *Book Two*

Fur-Given Book *Three*

Tigers

Stripe-Tease *Book Four*

Stripe-Search *Book Five*

Stripe-Club *Book Six*

Alien Warriors

The Alien Warrior's Woman *Book One*

The Alien's Rebel *Book Two*

ALSO BY MILLY TAIDEN

Other Works

The Hunt

Wynters Captive

Every Witch Way

Hex and Sex Set

Alpha Owned

Match Made in Hell

Wolf Fever

ALSO BY MILLY TAIDEN

HOWLS Romances

The Wolf's Royal Baby

The Wolf's Bandit

Goldie and the Bears

Her Fairytale Wolf *Co-Written*

The Wolf's Dream Mate *Co-Written*

Her Winter Wolves *Co-Written*

The Alpha's Chase *Co-Written*

**If you have a teen or know someone who
might enjoy the CLEAN and SWEET Crystal
Kingdom books by Milly Taiden, try these:**

The Crystal Kingdom (CLEAN AND SWEET)

Fae Queen *Book One*

Elf Queen *Book Two*

Dark Queen *Book Three*

Fire Queen *Book Four*

If you enjoyed the book, please consider leaving a review, even if it's only a line or two; it would make all the difference and would be very much appreciated.

Thank you!

Printed in Poland
by Amazon Fulfillment
Poland Sp. z o.o., Wrocław

55987795R00190